CLICK

CLICK

BY

LINDA SUE PARK

DAVID ALMOND

EOIN COLFER

DEBORAH ELLIS

NICK HORNBY

RODDY DOYLE

TIM WYNNE-JONES

RUTH OZEKI

MARGO LANAGAN

GREGORY MAGUIRE

SCHOLASTIC

Scholastic Children's Books
A division of Scholastic Ltd
Euston House, 24 Eversholt Street
London, NW1 1DB, UK
Registered office: Westfield Road, Southam, Warwickshire, CV47 0RA
SCHOLASTIC and associated logos are trademarks and or registered trademarks
of Scholastic Inc.

First published in the US in 2007 by Arthur A. Levine Books,
an imprint of Scholastic Inc.
This edition published in the UK by Scholastic Ltd, 2007

Text copyright © 2007 by Linda Sue Park, David Almond, Eoin Colfer, Deborah Ellis, Nick
Hornby, Roddy Doyle, Tim Wynne-Jones, Ruth Ozeki, Margo Lanagan and Gregory Maguire

The right of Linda Sue Park, David Almond, Eoin Colfer, Deborah Ellis, Nick Hornby, Roddy
Doyle, Tim Wynne-Jones, Ruth Ozeki, Margo Lanagan and Gregory Maguire to be identified as
the authors of this work has been asserted by them.

10 digit ISBN 1 407 10591 4
13 digit ISBN 978 1407 10591 8

British Library Cataloguing-in-Publication Data
A CIP catalogue record for this book is available from the British Library

Reprinted by Scholastic India Pvt. Ltd., June 2009

This is a work of fiction. Names, characters, places, incidents and dialogues are products of the
author's imagination or are used fictitiously. Any resemblance to actual people, living or dead,
events or locales is entirely coincidental.

www.scholastic.co.uk/zone

Printed at India Binding House, Noida

CONTENTS

Chapter 1
MAGGIE

"I can't *believe* you're not going to open it!" Jason said. "Don't you want to know what it is?"

Maggie tightened her hands around the brown-paper-wrapped parcel on her lap. It was a little smaller than a shoebox, and yes, she did want to know what it was –

– *But not here. Not now, with Mom and Dad and Jason all staring at me. . . I need to be by myself. And I need to be on the couch.*

"C'mon, Mags." Jason changed his tone to a wheedle. "You got to see mine."

He'd opened his gift right away – a bunch of photos of famous sports stars. *Really* famous – people like Tiger Woods and Lance Armstrong and Michael Jordan, all the photos autographed with a personal message to Jason. Gee must have been collecting them for years.

Grandpa Gee, a photojournalist. For almost fifty years he'd travelled all around the world taking pictures. War. Nature. People. Sports. There was no subject he wasn't interested in. His real name was George – George Keane – but he'd always signed his photos G. Keane, so everyone called him Gee.

Jason and Maggie were Henschlers – Gee was Mom's father – but Gee's name was part of theirs. Jason Keane Henschler and Margaret Keane Henschler. Maggie liked that Keane was her middle name, not hyphenated. She loved Dad's family too, but in her heart – in the middle of her – she felt like she was mostly Keane.

Mom and Dad had been to see Gee's lawyer and brought back the gifts Gee had left to Jason and Maggie in his will.

"Jason," Dad said, "Maggie's call."

"Yeah, yeah," Jason muttered.

Maggie looked at Dad gratefully. Then she took her parcel and went to sit on the couch in the study, where she'd been spending most of her time since the funeral.

After the service, the house had been full of people and food – why did people always bring food when somebody died? Maggie sure as heck hadn't felt like eating. It was nice of them, but she'd had to get away from all those people looking at her sorrowfully, the sympathetic murmurs – *He and Maggie were really close. Poor little thing.*

So she'd slipped into the study and closed the door. She'd fallen asleep there on the couch, waking the next morning to find that someone, probably Mom, had covered her with a blanket but otherwise left her undisturbed.

Now, three days after the funeral, Maggie was sort of living on the couch. Not *all* the time, of course. She had to leave it to go to school, to go to the bathroom, to fetch something from another room. But otherwise she stayed curled up on the right cushion, where Gee had always sat. She did her homework there, listened to music, read, sometimes hearing the back door bang as Jason came and went. She ate dinner from a tray. Every evening Mom stuck her head in the door and said, "You all right?" Maggie would nod wordlessly; Mom would look at her for a few moments, then sigh and disappear.

Maggie put the parcel down carefully on the lamp table next to the couch. She sat down and picked at a loose thread on the worn tweed seat cushion.

Nobody understands.

Mom with her new job, now that Maggie was in junior high and old enough to look after herself. Dad and his fancy promotion, away so often at conferences and meetings. Jason, a big-shot senior, always busy with his friends and his after-school job and never any time to hang around the house. Gee had been the only one in the family who had listened, really listened, to Maggie. Their story swap, her favourite thing ever.

And he had to go and die on her.

A heart attack, no warning. At least none that she knew about. Mom said later that Gee had called and mentioned feeling tired, but Maggie hadn't thought anything about it at the time. A week later, he was gone.

Maggie sat on the couch, staring at the parcel. She picked it up and shook it gently to hear a faint rattle. Then she turned it over and lifted the first piece of tape.

No. When I open it, it will be like my very last contact with Gee.

Not yet.

She pressed the tape back in place.

Maggie couldn't remember a time without Gee's visits. Mom would say, "Gee's coming over tonight." Gee, back from one of his many trips to far-off places, always came to see Maggie's family on his first night home, always right around eight o'clock.

Maggie would watch for him. As a toddler, standing on the couch to see over its back out the window. A little older, climbing to sit on the couch's upright cushions – the one in the middle still saggy from those years.

When she saw his car coming down the street, she'd bounce off the couch and run to the front door. She had to be standing on the porch before Gee was out of the car. That was the rule. They'd go into the house, where Gee would say hello to the rest of the family. They'd chat for a few minutes while Maggie waited.

Then Gee and Maggie would go into the study and sit on the couch for the story swap. Gee always had lots of stories about the strange and beautiful places he'd been. But before he'd tell her anything, Maggie had to tell *him* a story, about something she'd done or seen or read since the last time they'd been together.

Jason used to join them too. Not any more. In the past year or so, Jason hadn't wanted to do anything at all with the family; it was almost as if he couldn't stand the sight of them.

It had taken Maggie a while to get used to the story swap without Jason. She realized that he had often said things during the swap that he never mentioned any other time. She couldn't understand it; Jason had loved the story swap as much as she did. OK, so now he had a real job that kept him pretty busy, but did that mean he also had to become a complete jerk about everything? What was the matter with him?

Still, the story swap had gone on without him. Whenever Gee was away, Maggie did her best to stay alert. To watch and listen, to try new things, to pay attention to what she read so she'd have a good story to tell him when he got back. No matter what it was – something that happened in school, a movie she'd seen, the recap of one of her soccer games – Gee always listened carefully to every word.

After Maggie was finished, it was Gee's turn. His stories almost always started out with a photo, or some little object that he took from his pocket. "Guess what this is?" he'd say.

One time it was a delicate cage of mesh and bamboo small enough to fit in the palm of his hand. "A cricket cage," Gee said. "In Japan and China, some people keep crickets as pets. To hear them sing." Another time, a picture of a girl about Maggie's age, soaking wet, her face turned toward the sky, her mouth wide open with laughter.

"Guess why she's so happy?"

"She's been swimming in the ocean." Maggie loved the ocean.

"Good guess. But no, something *way* better than that. It's the first time it's rained in her village in almost two years."

When Maggie was little, Gee's stories were always about things that were funny or pretty or nice. Lately, though, some of his stories had been different. Like with the photo of the wet-faced girl. It had been last year – in the spring, maybe? After they had looked at the photo together, Gee put it on the coffee table in front of them. He was silent for a few moments. He started to speak, stopped, and was quiet again.

Then he looked at Maggie – hard, like he was trying to see through her eyes right into her brain. Maggie was puzzled but stared right back, trying not to blink.

Finally Gee glanced down at the photo and began to speak. "The people in this village – they had to keep moving to find water," he said. "They would walk for miles and miles. Most of the time, the water they found was bad – dirty, full of germs. But they drank it anyway – it was so hot, a hundred twenty degrees sometimes, and they were so thirsty. . ."

A pause. Gee was looking at the picture, but Maggie could tell that he was seeing something else in his mind. "This girl, she had a brother. Just a little guy, maybe three or four years old. Wouldn't let me take his picture. He'd hide his face whenever he saw me coming." Gee shook his head. "I really wanted to – he had a great face. But I finally had to give up, he was that stubborn."

Gee cleared his throat. "He got parasites from drinking the water. I mean, he wasn't the only one who got them, but he was so little, he wasn't strong enough. . . Two days after the rain came – two days after I took that picture of his sister there – he died."

He hunched his shoulders. "Should have shot him any-way," he muttered, so quietly that Maggie could barely hear him. "Stupid. I could have done it so he never noticed. . ."

Maggie stared at the photo. The girl was still laughing, but now some of the drops on her face looked like tears.

Maggie knew that Gee wouldn't have told her that part of the story, about the brother, when she was younger. Even though she was mostly sad when he told her, one corner of her mind had been a little proud too. She had decided it meant that she was growing up – that Gee thought she was old enough to hear the stories underneath the stories.

Now, as she sat alone on the couch, a wave of what she could only think of as fear came over her. If Gee's stories had been helping her grow up, and now there wouldn't be any more –

She felt like falling into a huge hole: the hole that should have been filled with all the layers of stories Gee would have told her if he were still alive.

So I might as well just stay right on the couch. It's safe here. Besides, what's the use of doing anything. I don't need stories any more.

Maggie let herself into the house after school and headed straight for the study.

"Hi, hon."

Maggie tripped, almost dropping her backpack.

"Good grief! What are you trying to do, give me a heart attack?" Maggie didn't mean to sound angry, but she was so startled that her words came out too loud.

What was Mom doing at home? She was never there when Maggie got back from school; she never came home any earlier than dinnertime.

"What's the matter?" Maggie said once she'd caught her breath back. "Are you sick?"

Mom stood up from the kitchen table and walked to the study door. She stood in front of it with her arms crossed.

"I came home because I'm worried about you," she said. "You're not going to sit on that couch all day. I know you miss him – we all do. But I'm here for you, and we can do whatever you want – go shopping, or to the library, or I'll take you to a friend's house. I don't care what you do, as long as you don't go into this room."

Maggie felt a weakness in her stomach that quickly spread to her legs.

"Why? Why can't I stay on the couch? I'm not bothering anyone – I'm getting all my work done –"

Mom didn't move from the door. She raised her chin a little.

The trembling in Maggie's legs turned into panic. "No! I have to sit there! You can't stop me!"

"I can and I am." Mom's voice still quiet but strong.

"You – you – why do you even *care*?" Maggie shouted. "You're never home any more – I'm doing *fine* on my own – why don't you just *leave me alone*!"

She wanted to turn and run. But the only place she would have run to was the couch, and Mom was blocking the way.

"Maggie." Mom looked really unhappy. *Good. Maybe she's getting an idea of how I feel.* "Please, honey. Tell me what you want."

Maggie hadn't cried since Gee's death. Not once. Not when they got the news, not at the funeral, never on the couch; the couch was not a place for crying. Now, suddenly, she wanted to bawl like a baby. Every single one of her cells ached to cry out, *I want Gee! I want Gee back!*

She swallowed hard, then took quick breaths through her mouth. Gee had always believed it was pure silliness to cry when somebody *old* died – "a waste of perfectly good tears," he'd said. Maggie wasn't going to let him down.

Mom waited for an answer.

What do I want?

"I want my present from Gee," Maggie said. "It's in there, on the lamp table."

Mom, still refusing to let Maggie into the study, fetched the parcel herself and handed it over. Maggie took it up to her room. She sat down on the bed.

A parcel from Gee.

Who had known he was going to die some day.

Duh. Everybody dies.

But this gift meant that Gee had been thinking of her. He'd got it, whatever it was, way ahead of time, and had it all ready just like he'd done with the photos for Jason, and he meant for her to have it after he died.

Maggie turned the package over, and undid the Scotch tape carefully.

Brown paper. A cardboard box. Layers of white tissue, and finally, wood.

A wooden box. Simple, but not plain; the edge all around was bevelled. Blond wood, with a dark grain of fine lines and whorls.

She ran her finger around the bevelled edge's smoothness. *There's something inside, I know there is. Gee left me more than just a pretty box.*

She lifted the lid.

A card on top. An ordinary index card, with Gee's scrawl on it:

Mags –
Throw them all back –
Gee

She put the card aside and stared at the box's interior. Two rows of compartments – four in one row, three in the other. Each topped by a square of wood with a small round knob in the centre. The compartments all the same size, the row of three flanked by pieces of wood so the whole interior was perfectly fitted. She'd never seen anything quite like it; Gee must have had it specially made. Or maybe found it somewhere, in a busy market in some exotic city. . .

A box of boxes. Maggie smiled, a tiny smile. It wasn't one gift. It was seven – eight if you counted the box itself.

She lifted the first little lid, the one in the top left-hand corner. The lid was polished smooth, like the rest of the wood. The tiny compartment was padded and lined with red silk. With two fingers, she reached inside.

A seashell. White and spiralled. Maggie examined it for a moment, then put it back into its compartment and replaced the lid.

The next compartment. Orange silk lining, and another shell. This one like a scallop, ridges beige and brown.

As she put the second shell back, she dropped the little compartment lid; it fell upside-down on the bedspread. Then she saw it – the letter A carved into the wood. On the underside

11

of the lid, where it couldn't be seen when the compartment was closed.

She picked up the first lid and studied it. Yes, another A.

Third compartment. Yellow silk. Blue shell. The letter E.

One by one, Maggie opened the little lids until she'd seen the contents of all seven compartments.

Then she knew for sure.

Gee had left her a puzzle.

Part of it was easy. By the fourth compartment, she'd known what colour the silk lining would be. Green. The compartments were lined in the seven colours of the rainbow: red–orange–yellow–green–blue–indigo–violet. ROYGBIV. Years ago Gee had brought her a crystal prism from Austria, held it up in the sunlight, told her the spectrum. "Roy and Biv, with me in the middle," Gee said, and they laughed together. That made it easy, she could rattle off those colours no problem, even though she was only six. The prism had hung in her window, rainbows skittering around the walls until just last year, when Jason hurled a stuffed animal at her – mostly joking – and she ducked, and it hit the prism instead.

Still mad at Jason for that.

Last shell, tan and twirly.

Maggie took off all seven lids, placed them in a row next to her. The silk linings looked smooth and shiny in the light from the window.

A box with a rainbow inside. Rainbows, light – light and dark always so important to Gee, to his work.

She picked up the card again.

Throw them all back.

Another part of the puzzle.

Back? Back must mean, back where they came from. The ocean. She could almost hear Gee's voice saying "Guess which ocean?"

The carved letters had to be a clue. Maggie replaced the lids carefully but upside-down, making sure to match each lid with its compartment. She'd kept them in order for just that reason. Then she studied the letters:

A A E NA

A SA A

Why so many A's? Does that mean four of the shells are from the same place?

A – Atlantic. Four from the Atlantic Ocean? And NA, North Atlantic; SA, South Atlantic? Six shells from the Atlantic Ocean?

That would make sense. Maggie's family lived in western New York. The Atlantic was the closest ocean.

When I was eight, and we went to Cape Cod. The only time I've been to the ocean. And I got an ear infection, so bad I had to go to the hospital, and the doctor said absolutely positively no swimming for two weeks. The whole vacation Mom wouldn't let me go anywhere near the water, not even to wade. And Gee was there too, so he saw how hard it was for me, to be so close to the ocean and not allowed to go in. . .

A box of seashells because she loved the ocean? It would be like Gee, except – except –

Something wasn't quite right. *Seashells. Throw them all back. Six of them into the Atlantic, and the seventh . . . E, what ocean begins with E?* Maggie couldn't think of one right off, but even if there was one –

It was too easy.

Not like Gee.

A puzzle from Gee – it would be like the box itself. Simple, but not plain. . .

Gee would have made a puzzle simple, but not easy.

Maggie ate dinner at the kitchen table that night. No meal on a tray for her; the study – and the couch – were still off-limits. Jason was out with his friends, as usual.

"Salad produced and directed by yours truly," Dad said as he put the big wooden bowl on the table.

Maggie stared. Blond wood with a darker, fine-lined grain. . . She touched the bowl, then looked up at Mom.

"What kind of wood is this?"

"Birch," Mom said. "From Gee. But I can't remember where he got it."

So my box is made of birch. I wonder if it's from the same place as the bowl. . . Maybe he took photos for an article about – about birch trees or something, I could try to find it in his files. . .

Dad sat down, raised his water glass. "A toast," he said. Maggie saw the glances, Dad to Mom and back again.

"What?" Maggie said. Picked up her glass but didn't raise it yet.

"I'm going to a conference in Japan," Dad said. "Mom and I talked it over –" pause, smile – "and we think you should go with me."

"To *Japan*?" Maggie heard her voice slide up the scale.

Dad nodding. "The Lees are going too, the whole family –" Dr Lee, a colleague of Dad's, two kids both younger than Maggie – "and Mrs Lee said you'd be welcome to hang out with her and the kids during the day when the conference is on, and we'll all get together at night. What do you say, Maggie-bags?"

Maggie looked at Mom. *Smiling, but her eyes aren't quite sure. . . She wants me to be glad about it, but it's so far away. . . I bet she wouldn't make me go if I didn't want to. . . Japan! Good grief, what a way to get me off the couch!*

It was the sort of thing that she and Gee would have laughed about together.

Maggie took a sip from her glass. "Can I think about it?" she said.

It would be six weeks before Dad left for Japan. Mom went into overdrive. Shopping for clothes, new suitcases, baseball caps and T-shirts to give away. "I'll be meeting lots of people," Dad said. "It's nice to have gifts for their kids."

Mom got books about Japan from the library, including one about the city of Sapporo (where the conference would be held) and Otaru, where they'd spend a weekend. Otaru was on the coast; their hotel overlooked the Sea of Japan.

The ocean. . .

Two Japanese language tapes – one for the stereo at home, the other for in the car. "Hello", "Thank you," "Please", "How much?" – the air was filled with Japanese words, and Maggie found she was learning them without even trying. Her parents made her go out with them one evening, for dinner at a Japanese restaurant with the Lees.

Mom was pleased about that, but neither the dinner nor any of the other frantic preparations mattered to Maggie; she couldn't even manage to feel annoyed about them. She went to the restaurant to keep Mom from nagging. She heard the tapes because she couldn't very well *not* hear them.

But most of her mind was still huddled on the couch. The only time her interest flickered to life was when she thought about the box.

Maggie opened it for the hundredth time, took off the seven little lids, stared at the shells neat in their compartments.

There wasn't any ocean that began with the letter E – she'd checked. The encyclopedia, atlases, the Internet. A whole bunch of countries did have an "Eastern Sea", but mostly they were called that in the old days and had different names now. And besides, there were too many – how would she ever figure out which "Eastern Sea" was the right one?

At Cape Cod, when I wasn't allowed in the water, Gee talked Mom into letting me walk on the beach with him. At least that way I could see the ocean, and hear it.

Maggie held one of the little shells to her nose and breathed in deep. *Doesn't smell like the sea, but still it makes me remember – the salt, the spray. Gee and me, picking up clam-shells. Who could find the biggest one. Gee won, a monster shell, big as my two hands. "A quahog," Gee said. Co–hog. Holding that shell to my ear, hearing the ocean two ways, the real sea in one ear, the shell's sea in the other. . .*

The seven shells in the box were all small, not more than an inch or so in length. *If they were bigger, maybe I could hold them to my ear, and they'd tell me where they came from.* Maggie shook her head. Silly little-girl thought.

She looked at the shell in her hand again. It was the shell from the last compartment, the violet-lined one. Whorled, pointed, a goldy-tan colour. *Wonder what kind this is.*

And then she hit herself on the forehead with her other hand. *Duh!*

The next day on her way home from school, she stopped at the library.

Lots of seashell books, thank goodness. Maggie chose three – one that had amazing photographs, a second whose photos were not as good but had more shells listed, and a third just in case. Back home she paged through the first book, hands warm, fingers fluttery.

She had decided to start with that seventh shell, the tan one. There were others with more distinctive markings, but this one had a large flared opening she thought might be recognizable in the photos.

Sheesh, how many shells are there, a gazillion? The book was organized by general types; Maggie's shell was clearly a gastropod. She groaned – it was by far the biggest category. She found several shells that looked almost exactly like hers, but not quite. . .

Here! The buccinums – it's gotta be one of these. . . This one? No, too many ridges. This one is closer, but too orangey. Tan, big flared opening, whorl on top, turn the page –

And there it was. Clear as clear, the photo showed the twin of the seventh shell, a velvety buccinum, Latin name, *Volutharpa ampullacea perryi.*

Maggie placed the shell alongside the photo.

No doubt about it.

She pumped her fist once, grinning, and began to read the information under the photo.

Class Gastropod, *family* muricoidea buccinidae – *there's a mouthful for you – found only in the Sea of Japan. . .*

Maggie stopped reading, stopped breathing.

She read the line again.

Found only in the Sea of Japan?

Otaru – on the Sea of Japan – unbelievable – Dad's hotel right on the sea –

Maggie coughed out a short, sharp laugh, then shook her head. She'd had a sudden vision of herself leaning out the hotel room window to throw the shell back into the sea.

No, I won't do it that way. I'll walk on the beach – Gee must have done the same, to get this shell for me. . .

Maggie sat back, her throat lumping up with love and wonder.

How did you know, Gee? How did you know I'd be going to Japan?

The letter carved on the lid of the seventh shell's compartment was an A.

A – for Asia.

Maggie knew now. The letters were for the seven continents.

Four A's – Africa, Asia, Australia, Antarctica. North America and South America. And the E was Europe.

Shells from all over the world. All she had to do was look up the pictures, and she'd know where each shell came from.

Throwing them back was another matter, of course. It was a miracle that she'd be able to throw the first one back in just a few weeks. . .

Maggie frowned. *Africa? Antarctica? Good grief, how am I ever going to get to places like that?*

Then again, a few short weeks ago she'd never have believed

19

she'd be going to Japan. . .

"I figured it out, Gee," Maggie whispered.

The answer to the puzzle was a wish. Gee's wish for her – that someday she'd get to see all those places.

It'll take YEARS – my whole life, maybe!

Her whole life?

Of course.

Gee had given her a present that would last her whole life.

Maggie picked up the little tan shell. She couldn't stop smiling. She'd throw it back all right – it was what Gee had wanted.

But she'd find another one. To keep, or maybe to give to someone else. It might take her days – she might have to walk the beach for miles – but she just *knew* she'd find one.

That would make a great story.

Chapter 2
ANNIE

Mum says that all things can be turned to tales. When she said it first I thought she meant tales like fish tails. I was wrong. She meant tales like this, tales that are stories. But this tale of mine is very like a fish tail too. This is about me and my mum and where we come from. And it's about the man from America who came one sunlit day and took the picture that hangs on the wall by my bed and shows the truth of me. His name was Gee. So this little tale of mine is some of his tale too.

I'm Annie Lumsden, and I live with my mum in a house above the jetsam line on Stupor Beach. I'm thirteen years old and growing fast. I have hair that drifts like seaweed when I swim. I have eyes that shine like rock pools. My ears are like scallop shells. The ripples on my skin are like the ripples on the sand when the tide has turned back again. At night I gleam and glow like sea beneath the stars and moon. Thoughts dart and dance inside like little minnows in the shallows. They race and flash like mackerel farther out. My wonderings roll in the deep like seals. Dreams dive each night into the dark like dolphins do, and break out happy and free into the morning light. These are the things I know about myself and that I see when I look in the rock pools at myself. They are the things that I see when I look at the picture the Man from America gave to me before he went away.

Our house is a shack and is wooden, white and salty. We have a room each at the back, with a bed each, and a cupboard each, and a chair each. We have a kitchen just like everybody has and a bathroom just like everybody has. From the kitchen window we can see the village past the dunes – the steeple of St. Mungo's church, the flag on top of Stupor School, the chimneypot on the Slippery Eel. At the front of the shack is the room with the big wide window that looks out across the rocks, and rock pools, and the turning sea toward the rocky islands. There are many tales about the islands. Saints lived long ago on one of them. One of them has an ancient castle on a rock. It's said that mermaids used to live out there, and sing sailors to their doom. We are in the North. It is very beautiful. They say it's cold here, especially the water, but I know nothing else, so it isn't cold to me. Nor to Mum, who loves this place too. She was brought up in the city, but ever since she was a girl she knew her happiness would be found by the sea.

We have a sandy garden with a rickety fence, and in the garden are patterns of seashells, and rocks that Mum has painted with lovely faces. Mum sells models made from shells – sailing ships and mermaid's thrones and fancy cottages – in The Lyttle Gyfte Shoppe next to the Slippery Eel. She sells her painted rocks there too. When I was little, I

22

thought that these rocks were the faces of sisters and brothers and friends that had been washed up by the sea for me.
This made Mum laugh.

"No, my darling, they are simply rocks."

Then she lifted one of the rocks to her face and showed
how all things, even a rock that has lain for ever on an ordinary beach, can be made to turn to tales.

"Hello," she whispered to this rock, which bore the face of
a dark-haired little boy on it.

"Hello," it whispered back in such a soft, sweet voice.

"What is your name?" Mum said.

"My name is Septimus Samuel Swift," replied the rock, and
Mum held it close to her lips and let it look at me as it told its
tale of being the seventh son of a seventh son, and of travelling with pirates to Madagascar, and fighting with sea
monsters in the Sea of Japan.

"Was that you who spoke the words?" I asked.

She winked and smiled.

"How could you think such a thing?" she said.

And she stroked my hair and set off singing a sea shanty,
the kind she sings on folk nights in the Slippery Eel.

She finds tales everywhere, in grains of sand she picks up
from the garden, in puffs of smoke that drift out from the
chimneys of the village, in fragments of smooth timber or
glass in the jetsam. She will ask them, "Where did you come
from? How did you get here?" And they will answer her in
voices very like her own, but with new lilts and squeaks and

splashes in them that show they are their own. Mum is good with tales. Sometimes she visits Stupor Church of England Primary School and tells them to the young ones there. I used to sit with the children and listen. The teachers there, Mrs Marr and Miss Malone, were always so happy to see me again. "How are you getting on?" they asked, while the children giggled and whispered, "She's dafter than ever."

Long ago, they tried me at Stupor School. It didn't work. I couldn't learn. Words in books stayed stuck to the page like barnacles. They wouldn't turn themselves to sound and sense for me. Numbers clung to their books like limpets. They wouldn't add, subtract, or multiply for me. The children mocked and laughed. The teachers, Mrs Marr and Miss Malone, were gentle and kind but soon they started to shake their heads and turn away from me. They asked Mum to come in and talk. I'd been assessed, they said. Stupor Church of England Primary School couldn't give me what I needed. There was another school in another place where there were other children like me. I stood at the window that day while they talked at my back. I looked across the fields behind the school toward the hidden city where that other place would be. It broke my heart to think that I must spend my days so distant from my mum and from the sea. "It's for the best," said Mrs Marr. That was a momentous moment, the moment of my first fall. My legs went weak beneath me, and I tumbled to the floor, and the whole world went watery and dark, and wild watery voices sang sweetly in my brain and called me to them.

I came out of it to find Mum weeping over me, and shaking me, and screaming my name like I had drifted a million miles away, and the teacher yelling for help into the phone.

I reached up and caught Mum's falling tears.

"It's all right," I whispered sweetly to her. "It was lovely, Mum."

And it was. And I wanted it to happen again. And soon it did. And did again.

There followed months of trips to hospitals, and visits to doctors, and many, many tries to go past my strangeness and to find the secrets and the truth in me. There were lights shone deep into my eyes, blood sucked out of me, wires fixed to me, questions asked of me. There were stares and glares, and pondering and wondering, and medicines and needles, and much talk coming out of many flapping mouths, and much black writing written on much white paper. I was wired wrong. The chemicals that flowed in me were wrong. My brain was an electric storm. There had been damage from disease, from a bang on the head, damage at my birth. It ended with a single doctor, Dr John, in a single room with Mum and me.

"There is something wrong with Annie," said Dr John.

"Something?" asked my mum.

"Yes," said Dr John. He scratched his head. "Something. But we don't know what the something is, so we haven't got a name for it."

And we were silent. And I was very pleased. And Mum hugged me.

And Dr John said, "All of us are mysteries, even to us white-coated doctors. And some of us are a bit more of a puzzle than the rest of us."

He smiled into my eyes. He winked.

"You're a good girl, Annie Lumsden," he said.

"She is," said Mum.

"What's the thing," said Dr John, "that you like best in the whole wide world?"

And I answered, "My mum is that thing. That, and splashing and swimming like the fishes in the sea."

"Then that's good," he said. "For unlike most of us, you have the things you love close by you. And you have them there on little Stupor Beach. Be happy. Go home."

So we went home.

A teacher, Miss McLintock, came each Tuesday. I stayed daft.

We went back to Dr John every six weeks or so. I stayed a puzzle.

And we walked on the beach, sat in the sandy garden. Mum painted her rocks, and glued her shells, and told her tales, and sang her shanties. I swam and swam, and we were happy.

"I sometimes think," I said one day, "I should have been a fish."

"A fish?"

"Aye. Sometimes I dream I've got fins and a tail."

"Goodness gracious!" she said.

She jumped up and lifted my T-shirt and looked at my spine.

"What's there?" I said.

She kissed me.

"Nowt, my little minnow," she said.

She looked again.

"Thank goodness for that," she said.

I fell many, many times. It happened in the salty shack, in the sandy garden, on the sandy beach. My legs would lose their strength, and I would tumble, and the whole of everything turned watery, and it was like I really turned from Annie Lumsden to something else, to a fish or a seal or a dolphin. And when the world turned back again to sand and rocks and shacks and gardens, I would find Mum sitting close by, watching over me, waiting for me to return, and she'd smile and sweetly say, "Where you been, my little swimmer?" and I'd tell her I'd been far away beneath the sea to places of coral and shells and beautifully coloured fish, and she'd smile and smile to hear the words loosened from my tongue as I told my travelling tales. At first, Mum was scared that I would fall and lose myself when I was in the water, and that I would drown and be taken from her, but we came to know that it did not, and will never happen then, for in the water I am truly as I am – Annie Lumsden, seal girl, fish girl, dolphin girl, the girl who cannot drown.

Then there came the sunlit day, the day of Gee. I lay on the warm sand at Mum's side. My body and brain were re-forming themselves after a fall. Every time it happened, it was like being born again, like coming out from dark and lovely water and crawling into the world like a little new thing. She was gently stroking my seaweed hair, and we were lost in wonder at the puzzle of myself and the mystery of everything that is and ever was and ever will be. I gazed at her and asked,

"Mum, tell me where I come from."

And she started to tell me a tale I knew so well, ever since I was a little one.

"Once," she said, "when I was walking by the sea, I saw a fisherman. . ."

It was the old familiar tale. A man was fishing on the beach, casting his line far, far out into the water. A handsome man, in green waterproofs and green wellies. A hard-working man from far down south, taking a break at Stupor Beach. Mum passed by. They got to talking. He said he loved the wild-ness of the north. They got to drinking and dancing in the Slippery Eel. He listened to Mum singing her shanties. He called her a wild northern lass. He wasn't a bad man, not really, just a bit careless and a bit feckless. He stayed awhile, then quickly went away. He was searched for and never was found. Charles, his name was, or said it was. To tell the truth, he wouldn't have made a decent daddy. It was better like this, just Mum and me.

But that day, I put my finger to her lips.

"No," I told her. "Not that old one. I know that one."

"But it's true."

"Tell me something with a better truth in it, something that works out the puzzle of me."

"Turn you into a tale?"

"Aye. Turn me into a tale."

She winked.

"I didn't want to tell you this," she said. "Will you keep it secret?"

"Aye," I said.

She leaned over and looked at my back and stroked my spine.

"Nowt there," she said, "but maybe it's time to tell the truth at last."

And I lay there on the sand beneath the sun, and the sea rolled and turned close by, and seagulls cried, and the breeze lifted tiny grains of sand and scattered them on me. And Mum's fingers moved on me, and she breathed and sighed, and her voice started to flow over me and into me as sweet as any song, and it found in me a different Annie Lumsden, an Annie Lumsden that fitted with my fallings, my dreams, my body, and the sea.

"I was swimming," she murmured. "It was summer, morning, very early – milky white sky, not a breath of wind, water like glass. Most of the world was deep asleep. Not a soul to be seen but a man in the dunes with a dog a quarter mile away. Nowt on the sea except a single dinghy slipping northward.

Gannets high, high up, and little terns darting back and forth for fish into the water, and nervy oyster catchers by the rock pools. The tide had turned, and it went back nearly soundless, just a gentle lovely hissing as it drained away, and all around the secrets of the sea were given up, the rocks, the pools, the weeds, the darting creatures, and the crawling and the scuttling creatures, the million grains of sand. And as I swam, I was drawn backward and outward toward the islands, and farther from the line of jetsam and my things. Rocks began appearing all around. A great field of seaweed was exposed nearby, stems as thick as children's arms and long, brown rubbery leaves."

"Were you young?"

"Fourteen years younger than I am today. A young woman, and strong, with strong smooth swimming muscles on my shoulders. My things were high up on the beach beyond the jetsam, a red plastic bag, a green towel laid out. I remember as I swam and dived and drifted that I felt stunned, almost hypnotized. I kept trying to look back to the red and green, to remind myself that the solid world was the world I'd come from, and that I must swim back again."

She smiled at me.

"You know that feeling?"

I smiled.

"You know I know that feeling."

"And as I drifted, I felt the first touch on me."

"The touch?"

"A gentle, tender touch. I told myself at first it was the shifting of the seaweed, or the flicker of a little fish fin. But then it came again, like something touching, deliberately touching. Something moved beneath. It moved right under me. A flickering, swimming thing, slow and smooth. And it was gone. Then I was suddenly cold, and tiredness and hunger were in me. I stayed calm. I breaststroked slowly for the shore. I knelt in the wet sand there and told myself that I'd been wrong, I'd been deceived. I looked back. The sea was empty. I started to walk up the slope of wet sand toward my things. A bird screamed. I looked back again. A little tern hung dancing in the air close behind me, beak pointing down toward the water. It screamed again, then wheeled away as the man appeared from the brown-leaved weed."

"The man?" I whispered.

"He was slender, but with great shoulders on him. Hair slick like weed. Skin smooth and bright like sealskin. He crouched at the water's edge, poised between the land and sea. He cupped his hands and drank the sea. He raised his eyes toward the low, milky sun and turned them down again. I could not, dare not, move. I saw the fin folded along his back."

"The fin?"

"I saw his webbed fingers, his webbed toes. His eyes were huge and dark and shining. He laughed, as if the moment brought him great joy. He cupped his hands again, and poured water over himself. Then he raised his eyes and looked at me, and after a moment of great stillness in us both, he left the sea and came to me."

"You ran away?"

"There seemed no threat in him, no danger. I looked along the beach. The man with his dog in the dunes was a world away. The man with the fin came out. He knelt a yard away from me."

"Did he speak?"

"There was a sound from him, a splashing sound, like water rather than air was moving in his throat."

"What was he?"

"A mystery. A secret of the sea. He was very beautiful. I saw in his eyes he thought I was beautiful too."

I looked into my mother's eyes. What did I see there? The delight of memories, or the delight of her imaginings?

"He was my father?" I whispered.

Her eyes were limpid pools.

"That was the first day," she said. "We moved no closer to each other. We did not touch. I saw the water drying on him, leaving salt on his beautiful skin. When he saw this, he lowered himself into the field of weed again, and he was gone. But he came back again on other early milky mornings when the sea was calm. The last day he came, he stayed an hour with me. He came on to the land. We stayed in the shade beneath the rocks. I poured water from the rock pools over him. He was very beautiful, and his liquid voice was very beautiful."

"He was my father?"

"I touched his fin, his webs, his seaweed hair that day. I remember them still against my fingers. That last day we had to hurry back to the water. His skin, despite the rock pool water, was drying out, his voice was coarse, his eyes were suddenly touched with dread. We ran back to the water. He sighed as he lowered himself into the water. We looked at each other, he from within the sea, I from without. He reached out of the sea to me. His hand was dripping wet, and in it was a shell, this shell."

She opened her palm. In it was a seashell.

"Then he swam away."

I took the shell from her. It was ordinary as any seashell, beautiful as any seashell.

"I'll cut the story short," she said. "Nine months later you were born."

"And it's true?"

"And yes, it's –"

We heard a click. We turned. A man was standing close by. He held a camera to his face. He lowered it. "Forgive me," he said.

He moved toward us.

"But you were so lovely, the two of you there. It was just like the girl had been washed up by the sea."

We said nothing, were still lost in the tale that Mum had told.

"Name's Gee," he said. "I'm passing through. Staying at your Slippery Eel. Came to take pictures of your islands."

He asked to be forgiven again. He took our silence for coldness, a desire to be left alone. He bowed, continued on his way.

"Please," said Mum.

He paused, looked back at us.

"We have few pictures of ourselves," she said. "Could we have the one you've taken today?"

And he grinned, and we came back fully into the world, and Mum asked him into our sandy garden for tea.

He told us of his travels, of faraway cities and mountains and seas. He said he loved the feeling of moving through the world, light and free, moving through other people's stories. Sometimes, he said, his photographs when he got them home were like images from dreams and legends. He laughed with delight at Stupor Bay. He swept his hands toward the sea and the islands.

"Seems like no time since I was in France. Now look where I am. Who'd've guessed a place like this was waiting for me?"

We said we'd hardly ever moved from this place, and for the first time, as I looked at Gee, I found myself thinking that one day we might move away.

He told us about America, and the kids called Maggie and Jason.

"You got the perfect gifts for them," he said.

He bought a rock painted with the face of a grinning angel and the seashell model of a mermaid.

He sipped his tea and ate his scone. He took more photo-graphs of us and of the shack and of the islands.

"I always take home tales as well," he said.

He winked at Mum.

"You look like you might know a tale or two."

That night Mum sang shanties in the Eel. I sat with Gee and drank lemonade and nibbled crisps. Between the songs, he told me of all the seas he'd seen around the world. He dipped the tip of his finger into his beer.

"An atom of the water in this," he said, "was one day in the Sea of Japan." He dipped his finger again. "And an atom of this was in the Bay of Bengal. All seas flow into each other." He licked his finger, laughed. "And into us."

I swigged my lemonade. I felt the Baltic and the Yellow Sea and the Persian Gulf pour through me. Rain pattered on the window at our back. Mum's voice danced around the music of a flute. We joined in with the choruses. We tapped the rhythms on the table. Gee drank and told me of his home and his family so many miles away.

"I'm happy when I'm there," he said. "But then I travel, and I find so many places to be happy in."

Mum's singing ended and she sat between me and Gee, and her voice was edged with laughter. At closing time we stood outside. The rain had stopped, the clouds had dispersed, the moon was out. The sea thundered on the shore.

"I'll do those pics tonight," he said. "Use nighttime as a darkroom."

He touched Mum's face. He told her she was beautiful. I turned away. They whispered. I think they kissed.

The man with the fin surfaced in my dreams. I spoke the watery words for dad. He spoke the airy words for daughter. We swam together to southern seas of coloured fish and coral, to northern seas of icebergs and whales. We swam all night from sea to sea to sea to sea, and when I woke the sun was up and there were already voices in the garden.

"Come and see," said Mum when I appeared at the door.

Her eyes were wide and shining.

"Come and see," said Gee.

I walked barefooted through the sand. There were photographs scattered on the garden table. Mum held another photograph against her breast.

"You ever see one of these things develop?" said Gee.

I shook my head.

"The things in them are seen at first like secret things, through liquid, like secret creatures glimpsed beneath the sea. They're seen by a strange pale light that shines just like a moon." He narrowed his eyes, gazed at me, smiled. "These are the secrets I glimpsed last night, Annie Lumsden."

Then he stepped away from us, faced the islands, left us alone.

I sifted the photos on the table: Mum and me, the garden, the shack, the islands. Mum still held the other to her breast.

"Look, Annie," she said.

She bit her lip as she tilted the photograph over at last and let me see.

There we were, Mum and me at the water's edge. Like Gee said, it was like I was something washed up by the sea, like Mum was reaching out to help me up, to help me to be born. I saw how seaweedy my hair truly was, how sealy my skin was. Then I looked away, looked back again, but it was true. A fin was growing at my back. Narrow, pale, half formed, like it was just half grown, but it was a fin.

Mum touched me there, below my neck, between my shoulders. She traced the line of my spine. I touched where she touched, but we touched only me.

"Nothing there?" I whispered.

"Nothing there."

I traced the same line on the photograph. I looked at Gee, straight and tall, facing the islands and the sea.

"Could Gee –" I started.

"How could you think such a thing?" said Mum.

I looked at her.

"So the tale was true?" I said.

She smiled into my eyes.

"Aye. The tale was true."

And I pushed the photograph into her hand, and ran away from her and ran past Gee, and ran into the waves and didn't stop until I'd plunged down deep and burst back up again and swam and felt the joy of the fin quivering at my back, supporting me, helping me forward.

I looked back, saw Mum and Gee at the water's edge, hand in hand.

"You saw the truth!" I yelled.

"And the truth can set you free!" Gee answered back.

He went away soon afterwards. He said he had a boxer to see in London and maybe an actress in Milan, and there was a war he needed to attend to in the Far East, and. . . He shrugged. Must seem a shapeless, aimless life to folk like us, he said.

"You get yourself to the States one day," he said to me. "You go and see my Maggie."

I gulped.

"I will," I said, and as I said it, I believed it.

"Good. And you can be sure she'll know your tale by then."

We waited with him for a taxi outside the Slippery Eel. He had his painted rock and his shell mermaid. He held Mum tight and kissed her.

I held the shell that Mum had given me.

"Is this OK?" I said to her.

She smiled and nodded.

"It's for you," I said to Gee. "And then for Maggie."

He held it to his ear.

"I hear the roaring of the sea. I hear the whisper of its secrets. I hear the silence of its depths." He winked. "I know it's very precious, Annie. I'll keep it very safe."

And he kissed me on the brow. And the taxi came, and the man from America left Stupor Bay.

Afterward, things were never quite the same. Things that'd seemed fixed and hard and hopeless started to shift. Words stopped being barnacles. Numbers were no longer limpets. I started to feel as free on land as I did in the sea. I fell less and less. Miss McLintock started talking about trying me in a school again. Was it to do with Mum's tales and Gee's photograph? One day I dared to tell Dr John about the man with the fin. He laughed and laughed. I dared to show him Gee's picture, and he laughed again. Then he went quiet.

"Sometimes," he said, "the best way to understand how to be human is to understand our strangeness."

He asked to look at my back. He peeped down beneath the back of my collar.

"Nothing there?" I said.

"Yes. There is an astonishing thing there. A mystery. And sometimes the biggest mystery of all is how a mystery might help to solve another mystery." Then he laughed again. "Pick the sense out of that!" he said.

He smiled.

"Come back in a year's time, Annie Lumsden," he said.

And of course it was all to do with simple growing up, with

being thirteen, heading for fourteen and beyond. And it was to do with having a mum who thought there was nothing strange in loving a daughter who might be half a creature from the sea.

Chapter 3
JASON

Grandpa Gee died and Maggie got a box of shells. Her brother Jason got a bunch of signed photographs. Maggie got short-changed, in Jason's opinion. Signed photographs were a much more valuable commodity. Shells you could pick up on any beach in the world. Even cheap diners used shells for ashtrays. There were more shells in the world than cockroaches, and anything that plentiful couldn't be very valuable.

Original autographed photographs on the other hand were worth money to certain people. It was what dealers called a niche market. It was amazing what some people would pay hard cash for. Old comic books, postage stamps with mistakes on them. Wood carvings done by some guy a million years ago in a volcano crater. Unbelievable. In Jason's opinion, money was only good for one thing: taking you where you wanted to go. Jason had a lot of opinions.

The day after Grandpa Gee's funeral, Jason stuffed the parcel of photographs in his pocket and headed for the door.

Mom was standing by the coat rack in a daze, and only looked up when Jason opened the door.

"Jason," she said, as if he'd just beamed down from the *Enterprise*. "Where are you going?"

"Out," replied her son brusquely.

"Out where?"

Jason sighed deeply. "Out*side*. What do you care?"

His mother didn't answer. Every conversation with Jason these days led to an argument. Her son could turn the most innocent of topics into a fight. One time she had asked him if he wanted a chocolate bar and they ended up not speaking for two weeks.

Jason shut the door behind him feeling angry at his mom and at himself. He missed the old days before they told him he was adopted. Sure, it was harder then. OK, they lived in a small apartment with peeling wallpaper thicker than sliced bread. But he had believed they were an actual family then, they were connected.

So now little Maggie wasn't even his real sister. Maggie was OK, he supposed. A little on cloud nine with her ponies and story couches, but OK. But she was the real daughter. She got all the attention and understanding. Frank was not his father and Gina was not his mother.

Soon none of that would matter. In eight months, Jason would turn sixteen; then he would leave them all behind to play happy families.

Jason cycled his ten-speed to the mall, hopping kerbs and skipping across low divides. The bike had been a *love me* bribe from Frank for his twelfth birthday, and it had worked for one whole week; then Jason began taking the bike for granted and moved right on back to truculent teenager territory. The old ten-speed now needed a major overhaul just to qualify as a piece of junk. The chain was rusted stiff in spots, causing it to periodically jump its cogs. The pedals were twisted inwards from one too many close calls with the traffic, and scraped the frame with every revolution. And the brake pads were no more than slivers of rubber that did little but squeak when applied. The Jason party line was that he was saving his after-school job money to buy a new Schwinn, but Jason had other plans for that money. That money was his getaway stash, and he would need more than a bike to get where he wanted to go.

Jason made it to the mall alive and stashed the bike behind the Brendan's Pizza rubbish bins. Brendan's Pizza. The worst name for a pizza restaurant in the history of pizza restaurants. Most non-Italian people who open pizza places go with evocative names – something that conjures images of Italy. Roma Pizza or Pizza di Napoli, but not Brendan Murphy. He reckoned that Irish people like pizza too, and a name like Brendan's Pizza might give him the edge in an evocative-name-saturated market.

Brendan was waiting for Jason when he slunk in the back door.

"Will you look who it is," boomed the big Irishman, making sure the other two staff members knew Jason was late. "The king of Kerry honouring us with his presence. His late presence."

"There was a pile-up on the road," said Jason lamely. It wasn't the first time he had used this excuse this month. Not even this week.

Brendan tossed him a pizza-wedge-shaped hat. "A pile-up? I have no doubt that you caused it. I'm tellin' you, Jason me lad, if it wasn't for your grandpa Gee helping out my family all those years ago, I would have long since tossed you out on your ungrateful backside. And now that he's passed on, Lord have mercy on him, you're my millstone for life."

Jason sighed. Another present from Grandpa Gee. First pictures, and now a demented Irishman. Thanks a bunch. Well, Brendan was wrong about one thing – Jason was nobody's millstone for life. In less than a year he would be sunning himself on Pigeon Point with his real father. Sooner, if the photographs in his pocket were worth anything.

"I wouldn't count on it, Brendan . . . Mr Murphy."

The Irishman twiddled his fingers before his face, and for a moment resembled nothing more than Oliver Hardy with flaming red hair.

"Don't tell me," he scoffed. "The Caribbean thing. Hunting for your real father. The dream at the end of a horse-manure rainbow you've been spreading for years now."

Jason felt the heat rising in his cheeks, as it always did when someone belittled his goal.

"That's not fair, Mr Murphy. You of all people shouldn't be laughing at dreams; you've got a pizza parlour called Brendan's Pizza, for God's sake."

Brendan picked mozzarella flecks from his tie, thinking about this. "Good point, Jason. But I never used my dream as a catchall excuse for opting out of life. How can anyone compare to a mystical father in the Caribbean?"

Jason cupped both hands around his eyes like binoculars. "Funny, I can't see any cameras," he said.

Brendan frowned. "What do you mean cameras?"

"TV cameras. Surely Oprah and Dr Phil are going to jump out of a tub of mushrooms any second."

The Irishman scowled. "Teenagers. You all think you have it tough. Let me tell you about tough. My family had to live through the famine. . ."

But he was talking to the swinging doors. Jason had jammed his pizza-slice hat over his ears and was out on the restaurant floor.

Jason was on tables that evening, which generally suited him. He would tune out his life, conjure up a cheeky grin, and put on a fake Irish brogue. The customers expected the accent, and it was worth a few dollars in tips. And every dollar was another air mile closer to Tobago. Closer to Pigeon Point. But today, Jason's life refused to be banished to a dark corner of his brain. There was too much happening right here at home to just dial it out. Grandpa Gee dying hurt him more than he expected. You would think that he was actually a blood relative, the way Jason had cried at the funeral. Then there was the constant battle with Mom and Dad. Shape up, stay out of trouble, blah blah blah. Every step he took was the wrong one

45

as far as they were concerned. Frank and Gina didn't under-stand him. How could they? They weren't his real parents. But at the funeral, when they huddled together under Frank's golf umbrella, he had felt something then, hadn't he? Comfort. Belonging. A sudden unwanted thought struck him. Maybe he shouldn't sell the photographs. Maybe he would regret it.

Jason scrubbed a tabletop furiously. They were not going to get him like that. Go soft at a funeral, and the next thing you know it's group hugs and sitting on the sofa with the entire family watching *American Idol*.

A bunch of people slid into booth three. Jason adopted his grin and hurried over, tipping the brim of his triangular pizza hat.

"Top o' the mornin' to you, folks. Welcome to Brendan's. Would you be likin' a Shamrock Shake before you start?"

"Begorrah, me lad, that's exactly what we'd be likin'. And aren't you the goodly wee leprechaun to be suggesting it."

Jason looked up. It was Aaron Biggs and a bunch from his high school. They knew him. They knew he wasn't Irish. This was one of the hazards of working in Brendan's. Sooner or later word got out, and your peers would make the trip espe-cially to sneer at your pizza hat.

Jason struggled to keep his smile in place.

"So, that's six shakes then?"

Aaron was on a roll. "Excellent, my little man. And if you could magic us up a box of Lucky Charms, that would be just dandy."

Jason's smile shrunk a few teeth. "We don't serve Lucky Charms, Aaron."

Aaron was undaunted. "Never mind, a bowl of four-leaf clovers will serve just as well."

His friends laughed. Jason didn't. It was going to be a long shift.

Aaron and his cohorts finally ran out of Irish jokes an hour and a half later. They hadn't even ordered pizza, and left a nickel tip. Jason ripped their paper tablecloth to shreds, stuffing it into the trash.

Tobago, he said to himself. *Tobago*.

He pocketed the nickel. *Thanks, Aaron. That will buy me a cola on the beach.*

There was an old bench beside the rubbish bins. Usually it was occupied by one of the pizza tossers sneaking a smoke, but at the moment it was empty. Jason sank on to the wooden seat, surprised to find that he was exhausted. Usually he could keep the cheeky grin going for most of his shift, but tonight it was proving difficult to maintain.

The envelope of photographs in his pocket dug into his ribs, so he took them out and laid the envelope on his lap. He wouldn't examine them again. There was no point in getting attached. As soon as work was over, he was taking the escalator up to Kronski's place for a price.

But after a few moments of looking at alley cats looking at

him, boredom took over and Jason pulled a sheaf of photographs from the packet.

The first one was a portrait of Michael Jordan, grinning like the cat who's got the cream, sunlight making a white circle on his shaven dome. Jason couldn't help smiling. Jordan was one of his heroes. He was one of everybody's, apart from the cartoon thing.

He flicked through the photographs. Tiger Woods swinging an iron. Eddie Irvine climbing out of his Formula One. Lennox Lewis jamming with a calypso band. There were dozens. All signed. All great photos. Jason had taken a photography module as part of his media studies class, and there had been a few of Grandpa Gee's photographs on the syllabus. Jason's favourite had always been a black-and-white shot of Gene Hackman resting his head against a door frame. He looked old and real and not at all like a movie star.

That's really something. To capture a moment like that.

Jason had another signed photo. A postcard from his real father. He had carried it around for the past three years the way some people carry a Bible. Frank and Gina had tried to track him down, but for some reason his dad didn't want to know him. They had asked for a meeting, but all they got was a postcard.

Jason put away Grandpa Gee's envelope, and fished the postcard from his wallet. The postcard from sun-kissed Tobago.

Jason knew Tobago was sun-kissed because it said so on

the card. *Greetings from the Sun-Kissed Island of Tobago*, in looping green print that ran across the card's top left-hand corner. There were eight people on the beach, all tanned and happy.

One was a boy, maybe six years old, wearing red swimming trunks with a gold anchor on the pocket. The boy was reaching for the sky, fingers curled above him as though he could tear grips in the air. His toes had broken free of the ground, and the skin was stretched tightly across his ribs. On his face shone a grin brighter than a crescent moon.

Jason could imagine how this photograph had been taken. "Jump," the boy's father had said. "Jump as high as you can, and I'll take a picture." The boy had jumped, and somehow his father had managed to press the shutter button at exactly the right second. And a moment of perfect happiness was captured for ever. Jason had never been to Pigeon Point. But he had a.postcard.

Jason often dreamed of this exact beach. The sand seemed so real that he could feel the grit under his toenails. He could imagine it now as the stress of the last week sapped his energy. The alley breeze cooled his brow, and his head began to feel as though it was made from lead.

In moments, he was immersed in the dream.

In the dream, Jason was working on Pigeon Point. Sitting on the keel of a bright green skiff, the paint flaking off beneath his fingers.

He was taller in the dream. Naturally. It would be a while

before he could save the rest of the money for the airfare. He was tanned too, and his sun-bleached hair was tied up in raggedy dreadlocks. A group of holidaymakers squatted on the sand before him in a relaxed semicircle, listening patiently while he explained the workings of an oxygen regulator. On Pigeon Point, Jason was a diving instructor with no past. A carefree young man who lived on the beach with his dad, and whose life was simple and good. He had arrived here one day with a duffel bag and no need to explain himself.

"If you get a blockage," he explained to the rapt tourists, "just press this button here, and that should clear it."

One of the tourists raised his hand. A blocky man with a triangular wedge of red hair.

"What do you do if you find some kid sleeping in the alley when he's supposed to be serving pizza?"

No one had ever asked questions in the dream before.

"What do you do if you can't fire this kid because you owe his grandpa a favour?"

Jason's dream toes wiggled in rainbow-soled flip-flops. He wanted to answer, but knew in his heart that it was no use. This stranger had robbed him of his dream of paradise.

He took one last look along the beach's crescent curve, then opened his eyes. Amazingly, the beach was still there.

"I found this on the ground," said Brendan, waving the postcard under Jason's nose. "Tobago. I went there once. Too hot.

How's a man supposed to breathe warm air? It's not natural. Like sucking on an exhaust pipe."

Jason didn't say anything, still one foot in the dream.

"I read the card too," continued Brendan. "I hope you don't mind."

Jason shrugged.

"'My dear Jason,'" quoted the Irishman. "'This is surely paradise. I have found work on the beach and I am happy. But this is no life for a kid. Stay where you are and be happy. Don't worry about me no more. We will meet again. Your loving father, J. P. Quinn.'"

Brendan waved a finger as thick as a policeman's truncheon.

"'Don't worry about me *no* more'? That's bad grammar right there, Jason. I don't mind bad grammar in conversation, but for a letter you have to make the effort."

Jason nodded for peace's sake.

"So anyway, young fella," said Brendan. "I came out here because your father called."

For a moment Jason's heart picked up its pace, then he realized that Brendan was of course talking about Frank, his adopted father.

"Your mother needs you at home. Her own father was buried recently, remember? I thought it was too early for you to come in."

"I want to be here," mumbled Jason, blinking the sleep stars from his eyes. "Need the money."

51

Brendan shook his head. "What is the matter with you, boy? Are you afraid to grieve with your own family, in case you might have to think of someone else for a change?"

Jason scowled. "You know there's a counsellor's spot open at the school, Mr Murphy."

Brendan slapped the corner of Jason's pizza-wedge hat. "Use your brain, boy. I'm guessing you have one. Look at what you have. Parents who love you, a sister as cute as a button, and Bright Spark here wants to exchange all that for some bum on a beach."

"Bum! That's my father. My real father."

Brendan spread his hands. "A man who leaves his kid is nobody's father."

"He had his reasons," protested Jason. "Good ones, I'll bet."

"Yes, like he needed to catch the next wave. Anyways, here are your choices – home or work. If you think that's unfair, then you should get another job. But no, I forgot, I'm the only one who will employ you after your little brushes with the law. So if you don't mind, your birthday party is here. Lucky you."

Jason didn't feel lucky. Winning the lottery, that was lucky. Having to spend your days in a crazy Irishman's pizza restaurant didn't feature on anybody's four-leaf clover wish list.

The patented Brendan's Birthday Bash included eight jumbo bacon-and-cabbage pizzas, a pitcher of green leprechaun shakes, and the Brendan's Pizza Birthday Song, composed by

Brendan himself and performed by whatever unfortunate waiter was working that table. This evening, Jason was that unfortunate.

He psyched himself up, wedged the wedge onto his head, and sauntered jauntily over to a booth packed with sugar-hyper kids and two tense and exhausted parents.

"Top o' the mornin', folks," he cried. "What can I be—"

"Pizzas 'n' lepr'chaun shake!" roared the birthday boy, his eyes wide with piglet greed and indulgence. "Pizzas 'n' lepr'chaun shake, funny hat man."

Standard stuff. Jason was not even put off his stride.

"Excellent choice, young fellow. Pizza and shakes it is."

The boy was not finished. "I want M&M's on the pizza."

"Brad, honey," began his mother, only to be silenced by a regal glare.

"It's my birthday, Mom. You said I could have whatever I wanted."

Brad's dad had a go at discipline. "Now, Brad. Of course you can have whatever you want, but within reason."

Brad was unbowed. "You weren't even here when Mom promised. You missed the gift semmony, 'cause of your meeting."

Brad's dad addressed the room guiltily. "It was an important meeting. People's jobs were at stake. I didn't want to miss the semm . . . ceremony."

"I want M&M's on the pizza and no milk in the milk shake."

Jason raised an eyebrow. *No milk in the milk shake?*

"'Cause I'm lactose intol'rant," announced Brad proudly.

This took Mom by surprise. "No, you're not, honey. You love milk."

Brad's face pumped up like a blood-pressure cuff. "My best friend Corey is lactose intol'rant, and so am I. It's my birthday and I can be whatever I want."

Brad's dad winked slyly at Jason. "Better make those milk shakes dairy-free," he said.

"Whatever the little master wants," said Jason obligingly, heading quickly for the kitchen. This was going to be a nightmare table. This was going to be one of those tables that waiters all over town would be joking about for years to come. But for now, Jason was finding it difficult to see the funny side.

He pushed through the swing doors into the kitchen, shouting as he entered.

"Six shakes for the birthday table!"

Eric the shake boy gave him the thumbs-up and began pouring from a large jug of blended ice cream and food dye.

Brendan was on the wall phone.

"It's Frank," he called. "For you."

"No time," said Jason, loading up a tray. "The birthday boy is a real drama queen. There'll be a riot if I don't get these shakes out."

Brendan relayed the message and hung up. "Frank was calling from the car. He's on his way down here."

Oh, great, thought Jason. *Just what I need. More drama.*

He pushed back out on to the restaurant floor, summoning up a traditional Irish grin from somewhere.

"Here we are now, folks. A round of milk shakes for everyone."

The children grabbed the glasses eagerly, slopping green gunge on the tabletop and each other.

"What about the birthday song?" demanded Brad, who had apparently forgotten about his lactose intol'rance.

Jason moaned internally. He was hoping to slide over that bit of the ceremony.

"Of course. The birthday song."

Brad slammed his palms on the table. "Shush, evvybody! The lep'chaun is gonna sing for me."

The table quieted down. As did most of the restaurant.

Jason cleared his throat. Singing wasn't really his forte. He could carry a tune for about as long as he could carry an anchor. But Brendan's birthday ballad was more about gusto than tuning.

Brendan had penned the words himself as a business ploy, tacking them on to the Irish classic "Danny Boy".

"*Oh Braddy boy,*" began Jason in a hopeful tenor.

Brad frowned. "Don't call me Braddy. Don' like it."

"*Oh Bra-aad boy,*" sang Jason, stretching the child's name to two syllables.

"*I hear the people calling,
From glen to glen and down the mountainside.*"

Brad frowned. "Glen is not my friend."

55

Jason ploughed on.

"*They say a prince,*

To Brendan's has come calling.

To celebrate,

His friends right by his side."

Most of the restaurant's adult patrons were groaning aloud by now. Jason didn't know if it was his voice or the suspect lyrics.

"*But come ye back,*

My happy little fellow.

Come every year,

And bring all of your friends."

Jason took a breath for the high section.

"*For we'll be heeeeere,*

With a comprehensive menu.

So order now,

For you must eat and I must fry!"

Jason thought his heart might pop at the end, but he held on for four beats. Two people clapped, and one of them was Brendan, who was clapping at his own lyrical genius.

Brad was unimpressed. "That song sucks. They got dancers and clowns at Burger King."

"Please, honey," said Brad's mother. "The young man is trying his best."

"Are you guys ready to order?" asked Jason, his grin a rictus.

The door swung open, and Frank walked in. It took him

about two seconds to figure out which leprechaun was his son.

"Jason, I need to talk to you."

Jason kept his head down. "Not now, Frank."

Frank's face was pale, and his eyes were bloodshot. "Can't you call me Dad? You always used to."

Jason's vision blurred. "I thought you were. But then you told me you weren't."

"Can't we deal with that later? In a few days. Your mother needs you."

"Well, what toppings would you like, folks? Just the basic bacon and cabbage? Or a few extras?" said Jason to the birthday group.

Frank persisted. "Do you know what your mother said to me? She said it was as though two people had died."

That one hurt.

"I gotta know the toppings," he said. "For the chef. Else you might get anchovies. And noooobody likes anchovies."

I have to get away. I have to get far away. The Caribbean. Tobago. Pigeon Point.

"Please. Think about somebody else for a few hours, son."

Then two things happened almost simultaneously. Jason rounded on his father of fifteen years.

"Don't call me that," he shouted in strangled tones. "I'm not your son. That's why I don't fit in. It's nobody's fault, we're just not blood."

And secondly, young Brad dumped his milk shake all over Jason's shoes.

The restaurant froze. Nothing moved but drops of green slop onto the linoleum floor.

Brad broke the spell. "I'm lactose intol'rant," he announced. "I tol' the lep'chaun already."

Jason looked down at his shoes, then up at the people he was serving. This could not be his life.

"Jason," said Frank, but he was beaten and he knew it.

Jason threw his wedge hat into the pool of green milk shake, and walked straight out of the door.

Kronski Antiques was an old junk shop on the third floor, up above the Gaps and Burger Kings – up with all the other small-time operators that couldn't afford prime spots. But the proprietor, Dr Kronski, wasn't like all the other shopkeepers on that level. When you came in the door, he looked at you like you were interrupting something important and he certainly did not need your business.

Jason had been here once before. Grandpa Gee had an old Civil War spyglass that he kept in a travel chest in their basement. Dr Kronski had given him twenty bucks for it. Grandpa hadn't even noticed it was missing. Jason had felt guilty about stealing it for a couple of days, but soon the feeling had faded from neon to dull. He didn't even think about the theft most of the time. Then Grandpa Gee died, and the guilt had flared up again like an infected wound, even though now his crime would never be discovered. He thought about what he had done every day, and the act made him sick to the pit of his stomach. Yet here he was back at Kronski's shopfront again. But this time it was different, wasn't it? This time he was only selling what he owned.

A brass bell tinkled as he pushed through the door. Jason could barely see the counter for all the junk, sorry, *"antiques"*, stacked on almost every inch of floor space. Whatever rent old Kronski was paying per square foot, he was definitely getting his money's worth.

There were harpsichords, and candelabras, and stuffed animals, and reconstructed battle scenes, and shrunken heads, and candles made from fat and blood. Of course Jason's brain didn't catalogue any of this. All he saw was junk that people would pay money for.

Kronski was behind the counter. A tall, slight man wearing a fitted black suit. His complexion was sallow, and his bald head shone orange from the overhead lights. He was busy painting a lead Napoleonic soldier, held in place with carpenter's clamps.

He glanced up from his work, brow creased with irritation.

"I really don't think I can help you, boy. Perhaps you are lost. There is an arcade one floor down." Kronski's accent was clipped. European. Jason didn't know enough geography to pin it down, but definitely something on the other side of the Atlantic.

Jason raised his face. "Hey, Doc. It's me, Jason."

Kronski removed a jeweller's glass from his eye. "Ah, yes. The light-fingered boy. The one with the spyglass."

Jason scowled. "About that spyglass. I looked that up on the Internet. It was worth eight hundred dollars; you gave me twenty."

Kronski smiled. His teeth were small and square, like an infant's.

"Eight hundred, with papers of provenance. Do you have such papers?"

Jason's silence was ample reply.

"I thought not. That twenty dollars was a finder's fee. Now, are you here to waste my time or to make some money?"

Jason turned his back for a moment, sliding one photograph from the package. It was a blurred black-and-white of two boxers in action. Their sinews were stretched, sweat streamed from their limbs, and their lips were drawn back over white gum shields. The photograph made you feel like you were ringside. There was a message scrawled across the top in black felt-tip. *To Jason,* it read. *You are the greatest.* And below that, a flamboyant signature: *Muhammad Ali.*

Jason stared at the photo for a minute. Grandpa Gee must have taken this photo in the seventies, and then somehow got Muhammad Ali to sign it after Jason was adopted. Amazing. Unique.

"What are you hiding there, boy? The crown jewels? Let me see, or get out."

Jason was suddenly reluctant to part with the picture, but

he conjured an image of Tobago in his mind, and it bolstered his resolve.

He slapped the picture down on the counter.

"What will you give me for this, Doc?"

Kronski took tweezers from a rack and picked up the picture by the corner.

"This is genuine, I suppose."

"Absolutely."

Kronski smiled thinly. "Let's say I get a friend of mine to check it out. After all, you are not known for your honesty." The doctor heaved open a leather-bound book bigger than a couple of Bibles, flicking through the pages.

"If it is genuine, then the almanac says I can let you have five dollars."

"Five dollars," gasped Jason. "But Muhammad Ali is a legend."

Kronski sighed. "These days, legends spend most of their time signing things. The average celebrity signs more than ten thousand pieces of assorted paper in a lifetime. I'll give you five dollars, or a hundred and fifty for that entire envelope."

A hundred and fifty dollars. Could he sell his inheritance for that little?

Kronski leaned across the counter. "Now, if you want to make some serious money. . ."

Jason felt his stomach churn. There was no way he was going to like whatever came next.

Dr Kronski drew the Civil War spyglass from a desk drawer.

"When you brought this to me, you mentioned an old box camera. I would really like that. I'm something of an enthusiast."

Jason's stomach lurchings increased in speed and intensity. All the old feelings of guilt resurfaced. He could pretend that selling the pictures meant nothing, but theft was theft, no matter how you looked at it.

"How much?"

Kronski shrugged. "A decent price this time. Five hundred if it's in good repair."

Jason calculated. With five hundred, plus the seven fifty he had saved, he could be ready to go on his birthday.

Kronski returned to his lead soldier.

"Think before you decide, young man. Decisions like this one tend to affect your entire future. It's not too late to go home to your family and be boring and happy."

Tobago, thought Jason. *Tobago. That's what I have always wanted.*

"I'm sure," he said. "I'll be back later. Count on it."

Kronski nodded thoughtfully. "I think you might."

Jason took the long way home. The house was in darkness except for an outside light that his mother always left on to guide him back. For some reason, the light made him feel even guiltier than the theft he was planning to commit.

He let himself in, creeping downstairs to the basement where Grandpa Gee kept his old junk. He stepped around the stacks of *National Geographic* and over boxes of toy cars from the last century. Grandpa Gee had almost as much junk as old Doc Kronski.

Finally Jason reached the old chest at the rear of the room and whipped back the tablecloth laid over it. The cloth snapped through the air and Jason froze, waiting for a reaction from above. None came. The house was as silent as space.

Jason opened the chest, searching the interior with a penlight. The camera was there, lying on the velvet lining of a wooden presentation box. And in the space left by the stolen spyglass was an envelope. The envelope was addressed to him.

Jason balanced the chest's lid on his forehead, reaching inside for the envelope. There was a letter inside. The handwriting was Grandpa Gee's. Jason recognized it from the dozens of letters he had received from faraway places.

Dear Jason, it read. *I am sorry for all the things that have built a wall between us. I am sorry that I am not your real grandfather, but I should not have tried to be. This lesson has cost me your affection and respect.*

I am sorry that there is no place for me in your world, because if there was, my life would be just about perfect.

I am sorry that your mother loves you so much, because

she will be heartbroken when you leave for Tobago, as we all know you will. Frank and Maggie will be devastated too. Like it or not, you are Maggie's hero. When you go, she will wonder what she did to drive you away.

Finally, I am sorry that you feel you have to steal from me. Do you need money for your Tobago fund? Is that it, Jason, my dearest boy? All you have to do is ask.

If stolen money takes you to a place, you will never be truly happy there. In time, you will be driven from the island by guilt. I know this is true, because I made a similar mistake once, and because you are a good person on the verge of a bad decision.

Think about what you are doing, Jason. We give you love, food, and shelter, and you throw them all back at us. And for what? For a father who deserted you. Can't you find your father without discarding your family?

This is my last letter to you. I have about a week left and a lot of people to write to. So my final gift to you is this:

Take what you need, Jason. I would not expose you even if I was around to do so. But think about the people who love and need you, and think about the road you are on and where it leads. Believe me, this advice is worth more than a few dusty antiques.

All my love,

Your friend,

G

The letter rustled slightly in Jason's trembling hands. Grandpa Gee had known all the time. He had spent the last few weeks praying for his grandfather's ignorance, and he himself had been the ignorant one. Grandpa had known of the theft, and the thief.

Jason dropped the chest lid. It crashed in the darkness, but he didn't care. He jumped to his feet, knocking over a stack of *Rolling Stone* magazines.

He had been so close. So close. Jason could almost smell the Caribbean. He'd stuck it out through funerals and Brendan blasted Murphy and lactose-intolerant kids. And now his resolve was being unravelled by a letter.

Take the camera, screamed his dark half. *Take it and go.*

But he could not. He was too much his mother's son and his little sister's hero. What kind of hero steals from his own family?

Jason mounted the stairs, putting some distance between himself and temptation. He sat glumly on the top step, head in hands. Now he had a new problem. If he was staying for a while longer, he had to get the spyglass back. How could he ever remember Grandpa Gee if he didn't retrieve the telescope?

The answer was obvious, of course, though it took Jason several minutes to admit to thinking of it. He had seven hundred and fifty dollars stashed in a *Lord of the Rings* boxed-set binder. His Tobago fund. The spyglass had been valued at eight hundred dollars.

CLICK

Jason trudged down the corridor to his bedroom. He would go down to the mall and haggle with the Doctor. He would go down tomorrow right after he had finished grovelling to Brendan. Maybe Kronski would do a deal.

Chapter 4
LEV

"Swill time!"

Swill time was any time. Lev didn't understand why the kitchen couldn't run on some sort of schedule, so that the food could arrive at roughly the same time every day. Late in the afternoon would be best, to give his belly something to work on in the evening, and his mind something to look forward to during the day. He'd even asked the guards about it when he first got locked up here. He got in return (1) laughter, (2) a fat lip, (3) no answer. Should have known better. Prisons, like orphanages, like families, like life, all operated without logic.

"Swill time!"

The voice was now right outside their cell door. No one else moved on their bunks. Lev was the junior prisoner in the cell, both the youngest and the most recent. His job was anything no one else wanted to do.

He left the bit of comfort his lumpy mattress provided and, keeping the thin blanket around his shoulders like an old woman's shawl, jumped down off his upper bunk.

The cell was small, and in four quick steps, Lev was at the door. The guard in the hallway unlatched the pass window. Lev put yesterday's empty pot on it, and received a full pot of food in return.

"It's hot!" Lev exclaimed. "The food is hot!" He didn't care that he was supposed to wait until everyone else got their share. Hot food was worth risking a beating. Anyway, the TB had sapped everyone's strength. A beating by those guys wouldn't amount to much.

The morning cough symphony started up as the other men tried to clear their lungs and catch their breath. Lev didn't even hear it any more, like the snoring, like living next to train tracks. He got his bowl and spoon, and lifted the lid off the pot.

Another surprise! Instead of the usual rice and cabbage gruel, Lev spotted potatoes, carrots, chunks of onion, and . . . chicken? And the smell – no, not smell. Smell was feet and toilets. Scent, that was the word. It was the scent of real food!

"Is it New Year's? Is it Easter? Is it the First of May?" Lev rhymed off all the holidays he could think of. The unfamiliar delicious scent got the others off their bunks, all except Vasily, who was too sick to get up.

"There must be a visitor coming," Nikolai said. He was senior in the cell, moving more smoothly on his one leg than most of his cell mates moved on two. He'd left his other leg in Afghanistan, and was well-versed in every scam Mother Russia had ever seen. "They always feed us well before an important visitor, so that if we're asked, 'What did you eat today?' we'll say 'chicken stew' instead of 'old vomit'."

"Maybe we should save some for later," Manchu said. His name wasn't really Manchu, but he came from Mongolia, which was sort of like Manchuria, so they called him Fu Manchu, like the bad Hollywood movies.

"It's hot now!" Lev said – not that his opinion held any weight, but he was eating his portion right away.

Kolya, from Omsk, near the Kazakhstan border, had turned Buddhist, learning it from one of the people he'd smuggled into Russia. Buddhism was bad for his business, but he was always the first to care for the sick, which meant that Lev didn't have to. Kolya left his own portion in the pot and spoon-fed the stew into the sick Vasily.

"You're wasting it on him," Nikolai said. "He is already dead."

"He still breathes," said Kolya.

"Then he's wasting oxygen too," said Nikolai. "I've seen death, and he's already there. Better to put a pillow over his face and throw the dice for his blanket."

Lev laughed and licked his bowl. Always side with strength, and in this cell, that was Nikolai.

The cell mates looked at Kolya's portion, still in the pot. Lev's belly was warm and actually felt like it had food in it, but there was always room for more. Stealing from new prisoners was allowed, but stealing from old-timers didn't make sense. They'd all need Kolya's nursing services before too long. Nikolai put the lid back on the pot to take the food out of their sight, and keep some of the heat in.

"He won't take any more," Kolya said, returning Vasily's bowl to the table. "A few spoonfuls, that's all."

Vasily's food was different from Kolya's. Vasily had been given his share and didn't want it. It was now up for grabs.

Nikolai did the honours, another scoop in each bowl. Lev thought briefly about the TB germs going from Vasily's mouth to the spoon to the stew, but what did it matter? Down went the food.

Lev was the youngest of the prison's incorrigibles, locked up for twenty-three hours a day. Other prisoners were let out of their cells to work, but not Lev's gang.

That didn't mean Lev didn't have chores. As the newest cell member, he had to clean the floor, wash the food pot, and clean the toilet. The taste of the stew remained with him as he worked. Real food was wonderful, but eating in the morning meant there was nothing to look forward to later, except maybe the visitor, if Nikolai was right.

"Who will it be?" he asked, interrupting a game of chess. Since there was always a game of chess going on, it was always being interrupted.

"Member of the Duma, Queen of England, Lenin himself, fresh from the mausoleum. What does it matter?"

There was no point in wondering. What would happen would happen. Most likely, nothing would happen. But it was something new to think about.

Chores done, Lev got back on his bunk and fished his project down from the little shelf beside his bed.

All the men had projects. Nikolai insisted on it. He said it kept them from going crazy. In addition to chess, cards, and language lessons, they made things to sell. Nikolai carved chess sets. Vasily, when he was well, made tiny churches out of wood chips. Kolya and Manchu made little statues out of chewed bread and straw, painting them with whatever they could find that made colour.

Now and then, a guard collected the finished pieces, sold them in a craft market, kept half the money, and brought back supplies and food. It was a rip-off, but that was Russia. Everyone out for themselves.

There were limits, though. A guard could be corrupt, but not overly greedy. Most of the prisoners were veterans. That brotherhood had long arms. A guard who got greedy was a guard with a short career.

Lev was making a box. He'd been working on it for the four months he'd been in the cell, and it was finally taking shape. It was small and plain, but every edge was smooth, every corner perfect. The wood came from the board under his mattress. He had no nails, so it was joined together the old-fashioned way. Everything fitted.

He lifted the lid and couldn't help feeling proud of himself. It wasn't just one box. It was a box of boxes, seven compartments, each with its own small lid.

Lev wondered what he could get for it – warm socks, chocolate, sausages, maybe some vodka to make the day slip away. Guards could smuggle anything in. All were luxuries, but all seemed too ordinary to exchange for something he'd worked so hard on.

There was noise in the hallway, then the door clanged open. "On your feet!" they were ordered. "Showers!"

Showers were so rare that everyone was slow to react; then they hopped to it, all but Vasily. There was hot water, and actual soap, and when they got out, clean trousers and pullovers – not new, but without holes.

The cell had been tossed. Vasily was gone. "Clinic," they were told.

"Can I see him?" Kolya asked, but the door was slammed shut.

Their projects were still there, but the lice-blankets and the bedbug mattresses were gone, and the cell reeked of disinfectant and bug spray.

Before they had a chance to get used to the empty room, the guards burst in again, with new mattresses, thick blankets, thermoses of hot tea, and even pillows! The guards placed these items without saying a word, then left again.

The four prisoners stared at each other for a long minute, then Nikolai said, "Well, I, for one, will take advantage of the warmth while it's here." He sat down on his bunk, preparing for a nap.

"Stay off the beds!" A guard opened the door, barked out the order, then closed the door again, doing it all quickly, like a bird in a cuckoo clock.

"Maybe it *is* the Queen of England," mused Nikolai.

The door banged open again. Men in suits, guards in uniforms, and one man with cameras around his neck crowded into the little room.

"This is a typical cell in the new Russia, and these are typical prisoners. As you can see, they are pampered compared to Soviet times," one of the suits said. To the prisoners, he said, "This is an American, from *Life* magazine. He's going to take your picture."

"Thank you," the American said, speaking clumsy but understandable Russian. "I was told I could speak with these men alone."

"They are dangerous."

"I have a letter. Would you like to see it again?"

The suits left, and the guards left, but Lev saw the pass window open a crack, and knew they were listening.

"When was your last shower?" the American asked in a loud voice. His mouth was smiling, and his back was to the door.

"Just this morning," Nikolai answered, just as loudly. "Hot, with soap."

"And your most recent meal?"

"Stew. Hot, with chicken."

"And what fine blankets you have." The American lifted his camera and snapped at the clean beds. Lev saw the pass window click shut.

The camera man rolled his eyes and shook hands

all around. "My name is Gee," he said. "May I take your pictures?"

"Why?" asked Kolya. "Don't you have prisons in America?"

"We have many prisons," Gee said. "My readers are more interested in prisons over here. If they knew about prisons in America, they'd have to do something about them. When they read about prisons here, they can shake their heads and say, 'Oh, those Russians!' then go have lunch."

"So you came here to help them feel better about themselves?"

"I came here to meet good people. I generally meet good people in prisons."

He got their permission to use his camera. He took group pictures, from every angle, then individual pictures. He took pictures of them sitting at their table, lying on their bunks, working on their projects. He asked for their stories, and wrote down what they said.

Lev came last.

"You are young," Gee said.

"I am seventeen."

"They put you in with grown men?"

"I commit the crimes of grown men."

"What crimes have you committed?"

Lev had to think. It had been a while since anyone had asked him that. "I've stolen," he said. Warm boots, raw turnips from a field, bread from a blind vendor's stall.

"Jewels? Cars?"

"You're making fun of me. You think I couldn't do it."

"I am constantly surprised by what people can do." Gee stopped clicking and set his camera down on the table to really listen. "Where are you from?"

"Abkhazia."

"That's in Georgia, isn't it?"

"That's a matter of opinion." War. There was always war when Lev was growing up. It got quiet, and he could go out in the street with his friends, then the war blasted up again, and then there was just running. Somewhere in all this running, his hand slipped from his mother's grip, and he got swept up with all the other refuse. Broken bricks got reused. Broken kids went to orphanages. It was the 1990s, and the world was a mess.

"You're a long way from where you started," Gee said.

"So are you," which made the Yank smile, so Lev smiled. He watched the American examine his project, taking the lid off the box, seeing the compartments inside.

"Why seven?" Gee asked. "There's room for eight. Why seven?"

"I would also like to know that," Nikolai said. "One for each of the men you've killed?"

"One for each time you've had your heart broken?" Manchu asked.

"One for each dream?" asked Kolya. "A dream is a sort of prayer. Is this a box of prayers?"

75

Lev didn't want to say, then didn't know why he didn't. These men had been kind to him, kinder than any of the other men and boys he'd been locked up with over the years. They might even be his friends.

"Seven escapes," he said. "Not the little runs. There have been too many of those to count. The seven big escapes, with travelling and a different life."

"Tell me," Gee invited, so Lev did.

There was the escape from his first orphanage, ending up with him as a stowaway on a fishing boat on the Black Sea. He was put into a stricter orphanage, but a ride on a chicken truck took him into Tblisi. He was caught stealing when he was living on the streets of the city, and sent to a training school. Over the fence, and into the countryside, where he was very comfortable in a barn until someone spotted him and started to scream. Then came the army cadets, where it was easy to take off into the woods and find a freight train to hop. A youth prison, then a medium-security place. His escape from there had landed him in here.

"That's only six," said Gee.

"My next escape will be my last. I won't get caught again."

Everyone laughed, but it was a good laugh, a cheering-him-on kind of laugh.

"I'd like to buy your box of escapes," Gee said. "I'd like to buy all of your creations."

Lev sat back while the others negotiated price and

payment details. They all wanted payment in advance, in a form they could use, before they turned over their projects. The guard cheated them, but at least he was a sure thing. Would they even see the American again?

Gee turned to a fresh page in his notebook and took down their lists – socks, long johns, something to smoke, things to eat, newspapers, a collection of Chekhov, a set of water paints, soap, and toothpaste. Things for survival, and things for feeling human.

"What about you?" Gee asked Lev. "Is there something special you want?"

Lev looked at the man, who could go on journeys and not pay a price for them, who could walk out of the prison and not be yanked back in. There must be something this man could do for him that no one else could do.

And then he knew what it was, and his mouth spoke the words the same instant they reached his brain. "I want you to find my mother."

A long moment passed between them, then Gee nodded, closed his notebook, and banged on the cell door. "I'll be back in a few days," he said. And then he left.

"That's the last we'll see of him," Nikolai said, and for the next three weeks it seemed Nikolai was right. The days crept by. A guard told them Vasily had died, and they held a little memorial for him in the cell. Lev kept expecting the good clothes and blankets to be taken away, but they weren't. The lice and the bedbugs came back, but the blankets were at least warmer than what they had before.

When Gee came back, he had his arms full. "The guards already got their share," he said, when the cell door closed.

"Rich American, showing off," said Kolya, but with a smile. There was fresh fruit for everyone, walnuts, sausages, tinned milk, bread and biscuits, a set of paints and brushes, the Chekhov and other books, warm clothes, everything they wanted and more.

Lev fingered the soft thickness of his new socks and put the soap to his nose, breathing in the scent of flowers through the wrapper. The food and amusements would make their time easier. He couldn't remember the last time someone was so kind to him.

Then Gee handed him an envelope.

"She was killed by a sniper," Gee said. "That's why she never came for you. I found your aunt. She gave me this."

Inside the envelope was a photograph. Lev saw his own younger face smiling at him from across the years. He was sitting on the lap of a woman he'd forgotten that he even remembered.

He handed over the box. The other men pretended not to notice that he was crying.

The American stayed with them for another hour, sharing their lives and stories. When he left with their projects, Lev's box tucked under his arm, Lev climbed up on his bunk. He put his mother's picture where the box used to be.

One more escape.

That's all he needed.

Chapter 5
MAGGIE

"I wish Grandpa Gee had been in the Beatles," said Maggie.

Frank tried not to sigh, but it was hard. Gee had been dead for over a year, and even now his daughter could suddenly come out with something like this – something that made sense only to her, something that showed that she wasn't yet . . . *right in the head*, he wanted to say, but Gina wouldn't approve of that expression. "Finished with the grieving process," Gina would say.

He went to the fridge to get himself some milk for his cereal.

"Do you want anything, Mags? Some more juice?"

"Because if he was in the Beatles, we'd hear him every day on the radio."

"We don't need to hear him every day on the radio."

"Don't you think it would be nice?"

"It'd be nice if he'd left us the royalties from his songs in his will."

Dumb, dumb, dumb. He never said the right things any more. He'd been careful in the first few weeks, but of course it had been easier then. Everyone was a little raw, and he wouldn't have dreamed of making silly little cracks like that. But a year later. . . Gee had been a great guy, a wonderful father-in-law, a terrific grandad. But life went on, right? Not in this house it didn't. Not in Maggie's corner of it, anyway.

"That wasn't what I meant," said Maggie sharply.

"No, sorry. I know it wasn't. I was just making a bad joke. What did you mean?"

He hadn't wanted to get involved in her madness, but now there was no choice. His little witticism about the royalties meant that he now had to take her seriously.

"I meant," said Maggie, "that he'd be a part of ordinary life, if we heard him on the radio all the time."

"He is a part of ordinary life," said Frank. "We remember him. We go to visit his grave."

"*I* go to visit his grave," Maggie said firmly.

"I've been."

"Once."

"Is it only once?"

"Yes."

Frank could have sworn it was more than once. In fact. . . Yes! It was twice! If you counted the funeral! He didn't want to get into a technical argument about this, though. It would sound a little undignified.

"It doesn't matter, Dad. That's kind of what I'm talking about."

"Is it? Good."

"Yeah. See, Gee's slipping away from us. Little by little, week by week. I thought I'd go to visit the grave every week. And I did, at first. But then it became every month, and last month I didn't go at all, which meant that this month I had to go twice to make up. . ."

"And you've still got the shells. Apart from the two you threw back."

A few weeks after Gee had died, Maggie had stood ankle-deep in the Sea of Japan one hot, jet-lagged afternoon and thrown one of her seven precious shells as far as she could. And then earlier this summer, Maggie and Gina had gone on a road trip to Cape Cod, Maggie's choice, where she'd thrown another one. Gee had collected seven for her, one from each continent, but Frank knew it would be a while before they got to Europe, let alone Antarctica.

"But it's all – it's all *special* stuff," said Maggie. "And life isn't full of special stuff. My life is school and friends and TV and books, and there's no place for Gee in any of that. If I want to remember him, I have to go sit on the couch and think about him. Or go visit the grave. Or get the shells out and look at them. It's not real. It's all. . . They're all New Year's Resolution things. You know. You always start off trying to keep them. But you can't, because they're not really *you*. I'm forgetting him, Dad."

Up until now, Frank wouldn't have said that this was the problem; he would have said – *had* said, to Gina, although not to Maggie – that the opposite was the problem. But now he could see that the recent little burst of grave-visiting and couch-sitting were about the forgetting, not the remembering. Maggie was trying to reel Gee back in.

"So you want to be able to remember him without making an effort."

She looked at him, trying to work out whether he was accusing her of being lazy, but she saw that he understood.

"That's right. Which is why I wish he was in the Beatles. Or some show on TV that's rerun every night, like *Seinfeld* or something."

"He'd have been great as Jerry's dad."

Maggie giggled.

"Yeah, well," said Frank. "Gee wasn't an actor, and he wasn't in a rock band. We have to work with what we got."

And then, a few days later, there was a miracle of sorts. Frank was at the kitchen table, reading an article about boxing – about how great it used to be, and how no one cared any more – in the sports section of the Sunday paper. And there, in the middle of the page, was a big picture of Muhammad Ali, of course. (Who else could it have been, in an article like that?) It was a photo he hadn't seen before: Ali after a fight, sweaty and tired, and a kid of twelve or thirteen with his fist on Ali's chin. Ali's got this great bug-eyed look on him, a look that's supposed to say, "Oh no! I'm not the greatest! This kid is the greatest." Frank looked at the bottom of the picture to see if there was any information about where the shot had been taken, but it just said "Photograph: G. Keane", and Frank felt a shiver up his spine.

"Hey, Mags," he said. "You were wrong. Gee was in the Beatles."

He pushed the paper along the counter.

Maggie stared at the name in disbelief.

"That's amazing! One of Gee's photos!"

"Yeah."

"This is just what I was talking about!"

"Yeah."

"He was like the Beatles of photographers, wasn't he, Dad?"

"Well. Yeah. Maybe more like, I don't know, the Mitch Ryder & the Detroit Wheels of photographers, but, yeah."

"Who were Mitch Ryder & the Detroit Wheels? I never heard of them."

"Oh, they were good. Some of their songs get played on oldies stations. Just . . . not every day."

"Cool. Not every day is OK."

Frank could see straight away that he'd made a mistake: Without intending to, he'd made a promise he couldn't keep. One of Gee's old photographs in the paper was already a message from God. But Maggie couldn't expect God to communicate with her on a regular basis. He was a busy guy.

For the next few days, Maggie was the one who went to fetch the newspaper in the morning; by the time Frank got to it, it looked as though it had been a small dog, rather than a teen-age girl, who'd collected it. Maggie had been through every page of every section; some of the sections were all muddled up, and some of the pages were strewn all over the floor.

"Mags. Most of Gee's photos were taken ten or twenty or fifty years ago. The photos in the paper were taken yesterday. Gee wasn't available for work yesterday."

"Not all of them were taken yesterday. Look."

She pointed to a picture of Ronald Reagan on the front of the "Life and Times" section, alongside a long and boring-looking article about presidential libraries.

"Gee could have taken that one."

"Yes, but he didn't."

"But he could have. That's why I keep looking."

"But don't look in the property section. Gee never took any photos of fancy houses, and he didn't take any photos of guys who sold fancy houses. And he certainly didn't take any pic-tures of weddings. Forget the weddings."

"You said he was interested in everything."

"He was interested in everything interesting."

"Weddings are interesting."

"Not to him, I don't think. He took pictures of wars, and boxers, and wild animals, and people who'd lived amazing lives."

"Why don't we have any on our walls? We could remember him that way."

"There you go. That's better than being in the Beatles. If

some of his pictures were up in your room, you'd be reminded of him every day, as soon as you get up."

What could be more simple? And who'd have thought that such a simple idea would turn out to be so complicated and so weird?

They began by going through all the pictures they had. They'd all been dumped in the basement after Gee's death, and no one had ever had the heart to go through them – or rather, no one had had the heart in the beginning, and as time went by, lack of heart had become lack of time and lack of energy. It was all such a mess – boxes and boxes full of newspaper cuttings, prints, negatives, bits of equipment.

"We've got to throw some of this out," Gina said. "These old lenses and bit of camera case and. . ."

Frank groaned softly. They should have talked about things like this before they got down to the basement. Mags wasn't in a throwing-out mood when it came to Gee. She wouldn't have let them throw out a used Kleenex, if it had been anywhere near Gee's nose.

"NO! We're not throwing anything—"

"It's OK, sweetie. It can all stay here," said Frank. "Your mom has gone temporarily insane. Jason will want all the photographic equipment, anyway. He'd kill us if we didn't give him a chance to sort through all this."

He looked at Gina, and she made a face and mouthed a big "sorry" at him.

"What are these?"

Mags was going through a little stack of prints that she'd found in an envelope. Frank half-saw the top one and then grabbed them from her.

"Hey! I found them first."

"I know, but. . ."

Frank had never seen these pictures before, but he knew what they were, because Gee had told him about them: They were all of Hiroshima victims.

"You don't want these on your wall," said Frank.

"You said I could choose."

"You can. Of course you can. But you know about Hiroshima and Nagasaki, right?"

"I'm not six years old, Dad."

"OK. Gee went to Japan soon after and took pictures of whatever he saw. There's some pretty upsetting stuff here. And maybe if you want to look at it, we should do it properly, not down here. We'd need to talk."

Maggie shrugged. "OK."

Frank breathed a sigh of relief. But Gee had been to a lot of war zones, he was beginning to realize; Frank had already had to hide several bundles of pictures, many of which showed things that would have given Maggie nightmares for weeks.

"What about that Muhammad Ali picture? You liked that. Why don't I phone someone at the paper and explain that we're relatives? I'm sure they'd give us a copy."

"Boxing is more a guy thing. Who's this?"

Maggie held up a picture of a beautiful young woman, apparently standing on the top of the Empire State Building. Frank guessed from her clothes and her hairstyle that the shot must have been taken some time in the late fifties; and though he was not by nature a romantic, he would have bet money that the young woman was in love with the photographer, and not just the camera.

Gina took the picture from her daughter and stared at it. "Well, it's not my mother, that's for sure."

"Why should it be your mother?" Maggie asked.

"Oh, just . . . I don't know. There's a look in her eye, wouldn't you say?"

"I can't imagine Gee taking someone to the top of the Empire State Building for a picture," said Frank. "Seems way too corny for him. Too touristy."

"What do you mean there's a look in her eye?" Maggie said to Gina.

"I think she likes the guy holding the camera."

"But that was Gee."

"Yeah."

"So she was Gee's girlfriend, maybe."

"Yeah. But. . ." She turned the picture over, and showed Maggie the date pencilled in the bottom right-hand corner: 6/15/61. "There shouldn't have been any girlfriends then. He was married. And I was born six months later."

"Oh."

"It's just a picture," said Frank. "Poor guy. He takes a photo of a pretty girl, and forty-five years later someone accuses him of being unfaithful."

"What about these, though?" said Maggie. She was holding a big bundle of pictures. Frank took them from her and flicked through them; they were all of the pretty girl. Or rather, the ones on the top of the bundle were of the girl; the ones underneath were of the pretty woman, the woman that the pretty girl became. Whoever she was, Gee had known her for the rest of his life, and had taken pictures of her whenever he could.

"He cheated on Mom," said Gina.

They were sitting in the kitchen, with coffees and a soda for Maggie, and Gina had spread the photos all over the breakfast table.

"You don't know that," said Frank. "He took a lot of photos of someone. That's all you can say."

"So who was she? If she wasn't his mistress?"

"What's a mistress?" Maggie asked.

"The girlfriend of a married man," said Gina. "Mistresses aren't nice people."

"Oh, come on, Gina."

"What? You like the idea of this?"

"I'm going to find out who she was," said Maggie.

"How?"

"I don't know. The Internet, I guess. I'm pretty good at finding things out now. I found out all about Sapporo before we went."

"Yes, but places are different," said Frank. "You knew what you wanted to find out. And you had a name."

"I don't want to know who she is anyway," said Gina. "What are you going to do? Invite her over for dinner?"

"Maybe," Maggie said. "She looks nice. But you'll have to do the cooking, Mom."

"Maggie, I don't think you understand what's just happened here," said Gina. "My life has just changed completely. It isn't what I thought it was. My dad wasn't a good guy."

"You don't know that," said Frank.

"Will you stop saying that?" Gina snapped.

"You're wrong anyway, Mom," said Maggie. "He was a great guy."

"We thought."

"He was a fantastic grandpa."

"And a great dad," said Frank. "You know it. I could find out tomorrow that my dad was a saint from the day he walked out our door, and it wouldn't make any difference to me. Nothing you find out now can make any difference to what your life was actually like."

Frank's dad was a drunk who had left Frank's mother when Frank was four.

"I just need some time, OK?" said Gina.

"Time for what? I'm sorry to say this again, but you don't know anything, Gina."

"You will soon, Mom," said Maggie. "Can I use your computer, Dad?"

Five minutes later, she came back to the kitchen waving a piece of paper.

"Her name is Jacqueline Aliadiere, and she lives in Nice," said Maggie.

Frank and Gina looked at her.

"But I've got to warn you. It's all pretty weird."

Maggie wasn't as stupid as her parents seemed to think. She knew that you couldn't find out much on the Internet unless you had some basic information, and she was going on her dad's computer with nothing. The thing was that she'd never Googled Gee before; it wasn't until that picture of the boxer turned up in the newspaper that she'd even thought of it. That was the first time she'd realized that Gee was famous. Not, you know, Britney Spears famous, but famous enough to get his name in the newspaper, even if the name was in tiny letters at the bottom of a photograph. Maggie and her friends had used Google for all sorts of people less famous than Gee. You could Google boys you liked at school and find stuff about them on the Internet. If a boy played for the school basketball team, then Google would point you in the direction of the school website; if his dad was an estate agent or whatever, then sometimes you could find an interview that mentioned his son on the company website. It always seemed amazing to

Maggie that the whole world could catch up on the tenth grade swim-team results, if they wanted to. Anyway, if you could find Sam Lander's name on the Internet, she was sure she could find Gee on there somewhere.

So she went to Google and typed in "'George Keane' photographer", and then she hit the "I'm Feeling Lucky" button, just to see where it would take her. And it took her to a website called "George Keane, photographer", and she felt all the breath leave her body for a moment.

The site was mostly a collection of Gee's pictures, hundreds and hundreds and hundreds of them. The pictures were grouped by decade and by theme, so you could click on "The 1940s" or "World War II" or "Vietnam" or "People". Maggie didn't want to look at the shots of Hiroshima or Vietnam, because she didn't want to see things that might upset her without her dad there to talk her through them. So she clicked on the "People" section first, and she found the Ali picture and pictures of lots of other famous people: John F. Kennedy, Marilyn Monroe, a baseball player called Joe DiMaggio, a lot of French actors and writers, and a photo of the pretty girl – one of the pictures they'd found in the basement. Under each photo was the name of the subject and the year it was taken, and so within two or three minutes of sitting down at the computer, she knew that the pretty girl was called Jacqueline. It had been so easy that she wanted to laugh. But she still didn't know who Jacqueline was.

And then she noticed a heading that said "About George

Keane", so she clicked on that, and there was a lovely smiling picture of Gee and a few lines about his life. She read the few lines, and that's when she went running downstairs. This George Keane wasn't the George Keane they knew. He couldn't be. This George Keane, it said, met fellow-photographer Jacqueline Aliadiere in Paris in 1946. And "Although he travelled all over the world, and made frequent visits back to his native United States, he lived in France for the rest of his life". He had one daughter and two grandchildren, and nobody was called Gina or Maggie or Jason.

"So there you are," said Frank. "He didn't cheat on your mom. He cheated on Jacqueline. And I mean, he *really* cheated on her, poor woman. He lived in the US for fifty years after the war and she never suspected a thing."

"It's not funny, Frank," said Gina.

"It's kind of funny," said Frank. "I mean, we're beyond cheating now. We're on the outer limit of *The Outer Limits*."

"We should go see her, Mom," said Maggie. "Jacqueline."

"Oh, I'm going. Don't worry about that."

"But you're going to take me, right?"

"I'm going soon, sweetheart. I'm not waiting until the holidays. You can't miss school for this."

"Put it this way. If you don't take me, I'll never go to school again. And you can explain to Gee that you could have taken me to Europe to throw a shell back, but you didn't feel like it."

And two weeks later, Maggie and Gina were on a plane to Nice.

* * *

Jacqueline Aliadiere lived in a village called Valbonne in the south of France, an hour north of Cannes. Gina had found an email address on the website and written, saying that she was writing an article about Gee for a photography magazine and she'd like to interview Jacqueline and look at any stuff she might have. She received a friendly reply from Jacqueline's daughter Chantal, in eccentric but charming English. Chantal explained that Jacqueline was fit and well, and she would be delighted to talk to Gina, but she didn't like computers, and took very little interest in the website. It was Chantal who had set it up, in memory of her father's work. Gina wanted to argue with her, of course. "Stop this," she wanted to say. "You're insane. He was not your father. He couldn't have been." But she'd save the arguments for when they got there.

Gina and Maggie rented a car at the airport, a bright yellow Citroën with lots of ashtrays and no radio, and they drove away from the coast toward the Alpes Maritimes. It was hot, and everything smelled different. Maggie got a few blasts of old drain, and slightly fewer blasts of pine or some other plant, one they didn't have at home. After they'd been driving for forty minutes or so and they had left the chic white hotels of Nice behind, Maggie decided it was much more foreign than Sapporo, which was only different from America because the writing on the high-rises and the fast-food restaurants was in Japanese. They drove through lots of villages that seemed as French as she could have wanted them to be – you could see the bars in the centre of the village, with old people sitting outside them, smoking and sipping their coffees. You could even see people playing that game with the big silver balls. It was as if the French didn't care whether they were being French or not; in America, they knew lots of people who would rather have died than allow anyone to think of them as typically American.

When they got to Valbonne, they parked the car outside the bar in the centre of the village and sat down at one of the tables. Chantal had told them to let the bar owner know when they had arrived, and she would come down to meet them; but Gina wasn't ready for that, so they sat in the shade and drank a weird kind of lemonade that was made from real lemons.

"OK," said Gina finally. "Let's get this over with." She went indoors to speak to the guy, and then they waited.

"Oh, my God," said Gina after a couple of minutes. Maggie followed her mother's eyes, and then saw what she was seeing. Coming toward them was a woman who. . . Well, it wasn't just that she looked like Gina. She more or less *was* Gina, give or take a dangly earring here and a grey hair or two there. Gina leaped to her feet.

"You must be Chantal," said Gina. She was trying to keep it together, Maggie could tell, and only just succeeding.

The woman looked at her, bewildered.

"*Pardon?*"

"Chantal?"

"*Je m'excuse,*" said the woman, and walked on past the bar

and into the *tabac* a couple of doors down.

Gina burst out laughing.

"How weird was that? She was nothing to do with anything. She was a red herring."

And then almost immediately, a small, fat, smiley lady, more or less the opposite of Gina, if people can be opposites, came up behind them and tapped Gina on the shoulder.

"Gina? I'm Chantal."

And Gina burst out laughing again, much to Chantal's bewilderment.

The three of them walked a little way up the hill and out of the village, and then turned into a gravelled driveway that led to a small, pretty little house covered in vines and set well back from the road.

"How was your journey?"

Chantal's spoken English was good and had clearly been learned from an American.

"Fine, thank you. Maggie here has never been to Europe before, so she's a little fazed."

"Fazed? Sorry. . ."

"Oh, you know. Psyched. Excited. Overcome. Overexcited."

Maggie looked at her. Sure, it was great to be in France, but she wasn't the one who was freaking out every five minutes.

An old lady leaning on a cane was standing outside the house ready to greet them.

"*Bonjour! Bonjour!*" the old lady shouted. With a great effort she started to do something with her stick.

"Oh, no," said Chantal suddenly, and started to run toward her. She got there just in time to catch Jacqueline before she fell.

"*Maman! Non plus!* I'm sorry," she said to Maggie and Gina. "She always is doing this. She wants to say hello to people by waving her stick, but it's her stick that makes her stand up." She shook her head, and both she and her mother laughed sorrowfully.

"Please. Come inside," said Chantal.

They were shown into a big room at the back of the house that was full of photographs and photography equipment. There were framed photos on the wall – some that Maggie recognized from the basement in their house, some that must have been by Jacqueline – and piles of photos on every available surface.

"Can I get you something? Some water? A coffee? A cola? We can eat later."

Gina asked for a glass of water, and Maggie accepted the offer of a Coke, and Chantal left the room.

"So, Madame Henschler," said Jacqueline. "You want to write something about my husband. What can I tell you?"

Maggie looked at her mother. Now that they were here, it was almost impossible to imagine how Gina was going to approach the subject that had made them travel across the Atlantic.

"I'd like some basic biographical details first," said Gina. "I mean, I know a lot of stuff. But I'd like to check it with you first."

"Of course."

"I read on the Internet that Gee was buried in the United States. Is that right? It seems strange."

"Gee?"

"I'm sorry. Monsieur Keane."

"You call him Gee?"

"Yeah. I don't know why. I think I read somewhere that people called him that."

"I never heard it before. Anyway. No, of course it's not right. He is here in the village."

"Oh. OK."

Maggie wondered how Mom could follow that question up. There wasn't any way that she could see, unless Gina was going to ask her if she was sure. And that didn't seem appropriate.

"When did he die?" Maggie asked.

"He died since a year."

"My grandpa died a year ago too," said Maggie.

"I'm sorry," said Jacqueline. "You miss him?"

"Yes," said Maggie. "Very much."

She wanted to tell her the day that he died, but it didn't seem right.

"He took photos too."

"Ah," said Jacqueline. "So you understand something."

"I understand a lot," said Maggie fiercely, and Jacqueline smiled.

And then everything went quiet. Maggie understood why. When they were back at home in the US, it was impossible to think of Jacqueline and Chantal as anything but crazy. But now they were here in France, it felt like they were the crazy ones. This Gee – Monsieur Keane – he'd lived his life here, and he was buried here. Maggie was sure of that. This woman wasn't shifty, or trying to hide anything. They weren't going to be able to trick her into confessing, because there wasn't anything to confess. So now what?

Chantal came back into the room with their drinks.

"I'm really sorry," Gina said to her. "But I'm feeling completely exhausted. It wouldn't be possible to come back tomorrow, would it? We have travelled a long way, and I don't want to . . . well, to waste this opportunity."

"Of course," said Chantal. "We're not doing anything."

Maggie was glad. They had nowhere left to go today. Her suspicion was that they had nowhere left to go, period.

"Mom."

"Yeah. What is it now?"

They were sharing a bed in the little guest-house that Chantal had recommended, and they'd both been trying to sleep for a while.

"How about this? You either believe in Gee or you don't."

"I'm sorry?"

"That's the only way I can explain it. I believe in Gee. Jacqueline and Chantal believe in their version of Gee. It's not like there's a right Gee and a wrong Gee, is it? Because there isn't only one Gee."

"I don't know."

"We can't come over to their country and tell them they've got it all wrong, can we? If they came over to our country and told us that Gee wasn't buried where we know he was buried, that you weren't his daughter, that he didn't live down the street from us for all those years . . . we'd want to punch them, wouldn't we? Maybe the important thing is that, I don't know, you've got some kind of Gee around."

"Maybe that's right. You're smart."

"Are you being sarcastic?"

"No. I mean it. That's a very smart way of looking at things, and I can't think of a better one."

Being smart didn't help Maggie get to sleep any quicker, though. Being smart made things worse.

Two days later, and the very next day after the four of them had had long and passionately devoted conversations about Gee's photography, Maggie was helping Jacqueline walk into the sea at a beach called La Garoupe, an hour or so from Valbonne. Maggie held Jacqueline's arm, and also helped her with the stick – every time the old lady put it down, it got stuck in the wet sand, and it took two of them to pull it out again.

"You don't think he'd mind that I'm throwing a Scottish shell into a French sea?"

"No. He was an American. Americans can't tell one European country from another. It's all Europe to them. How far out do you want to go?" Jacqueline asked.

"This is good," said Maggie. "Do you want to do it?"

"No," said Jacqueline. "Your grandfather wanted you to do it. You must do it."

Maggie was glad she'd turned down the offer. She would have felt bad. She felt around in her jeans pocket for the little shell, and then pulled it out to show the old lady.

"There."

"*Très jolie.* My husband liked to collect these."

"I thought he might," said Maggie.

She drew her arm back and threw the shell as far as she could, and watched it for as long as she could.

"Did you see it touch the water?" Jacqueline asked.

"Oh, yes," said Maggie. But she hadn't, she didn't think. She just wished she had.

Chapter 6
VINCENT

Vincent Sheils had two main claims to fame. He could put his left leg behind his head and stick the big toe into his right ear. And he'd once met Muhammad Ali.

But the last time he'd done the leg-behind-the-head trick his leg had refused to come back down, and an ambulance had come and taken him to Beaumont Hospital, where he'd had to lie on a trolley for seventeen hours before a doctor came and laughed at him.

"I've always been able to do it," he'd told the doctor, his head poking out of the cave that was his bent left leg. He was wearing shorts and the leg hair tickled his nose.

"What age are you, Mr Sheils?" asked the doctor.

"Forty-five," said Vincent. "It's my birthday."

"Happy birthday, Mr Sheils."

"Thank you, Doctor."

"May I suggest that you do not attempt this trick on your forty-sixth birthday?" said the doctor.

Vincent nodded and the pain shot down his spine, down and around his left leg, to the big toe and his right ear and into his brain. And it started all over again and would have gone on for the rest of his life if the doctor hadn't pulled the toe out of his ear and broken the circuit.

"Thank you, Doctor."

"You're welcome."

Now, two years later, Vincent still had two main claims to fame. He was the eejit who'd once spent seventeen hours on a hospital trolley, looking as if he was trying to climb up his own bum. And he'd once met Muhammad Ali.

His kids had grown up knowing the story. Of how, when he was fourteen, Vincent had met the legendary boxer, the great Ali, the greatest sportsman of the twentieth century.

"He let me punch him."

"Did you hurt him, Da?"

"Not at all. It was like thumping a wall.'"

They all knew the story but, over the years, it had meant less and less to them. His youngest children hardly knew who Ali was. Ali had retired a long time ago, and boxing wasn't the huge sport it had been when Vincent was a kid. The children had stopped asking to hear Vincent's story, and it had been kind of forgotten about.

But that had changed the night they all watched the opening ceremony of the Special Olympics on the telly. This was in 2003, when the Special Olympics were held in Dublin. The opening ceremony was in Croke Park, where Ali had fought in 1972, and very near where Vincent had grown up. They watched competitors from all over the world as they walked into the stadium, or came in wheelchairs. The cheering was incredible; it never stopped. More and more competitors filled the stadium. There were famous sports people and celebrities marching with the competitors – Colin Farrell, the actor; Roy Keane, the soccer player; and some singer with mad hair who Vincent had never heard of.

Then the cheering got even louder and they saw the shaking man. He was sitting on a trolley like a golf cart, and he came out with the American team. He was smiling, and waving; shaking.

"That's him," said Vincent. "That's Muhammad Ali."

Vincent's kids said nothing at first. They knew they were looking at someone very special.

"Why's he like that?" asked his youngest, Gavin.

"He has Parkinson's," said Vincent.

"What's that?"

"I think it means he can't control his muscles," said Vincent.

"That's sad, isn't it?"

"Yes," said Vincent.

"Could he control his muscles the day you hit him, Da?"

"Yes," said Vincent. "He was much younger."

"He looks nice," said his daughter, Ciara.

They looked at the crowd standing and clapping as Ali passed them on the cart.

"Was he nice the day you met him, Da?"

"Yeah," said Vincent. "He was."

Ciara touched the little scar on Vincent's forehead.

"Tell us."

And this time they listened.

Vinnie Sheils and his best friend, Frankie Shepherd, held on to the bar at the back of the bus. The bus conductor, the man who collected the bus fares from the passengers, was on the platform with them, having a smoke. He was known as Giggles, because he was always so miserable.

"He has a hard life," said Vinnie's ma once.

This was at their dinner, just after Giggles had knocked on the door and complained that Vinnie hadn't paid his bus fare to school that morning.

"What's so hard about collecting bus fares?" said his da.

"It's his wife," his ma whispered.

"What?" said his da. "Did she not pay her fare either?"

"Shhh."

Anyway, this day Vinnie and Frankie had paid their fare, so Giggles didn't care when he saw them jumping off the bus while it was still moving.

They jumped, Vinnie first, and ran alongside the bus until their legs were steady again, and they knew they weren't going to fall.

"Seeyeh, Giggles."

Frankie waved at the bus as he ran. That was why he didn't see the box of apples outside Cooney's shop, and he ran straight into it. Frankie was on the ground, the apples all around him. Old man Cooney was trying to grab his T-shirt and Cooney's daughter, Gertie, was attacking him with a brush.

"Does he have a licence for that daughter of his?" said Vinnie's da, once.

This was at their dinner, just after Cooney had knocked on the door and complained that Vinnie had robbed an orange and a bag of monkey nuts.

"God love her," said his ma. "She has a hard life."

That was the world according to Vinnie's ma: life was hard for everyone.

It was hard for Frankie anyway. There was blood pouring from his lip, and Gertie was standing right over him.

"Get your blood off our apples!" she shouted.

She swung the brush again, hard, and it hit Frankie in a place that really hurt.

And that, really, was why they didn't notice the man with the cameras. They were running past the church railings, getting away from Gertie and Cooney.

"I'm telling your mammies! I'm telling your mammies!"

Something caught the corner of Vinnie's eye, like the sun on a mirror. He looked, and saw the man on the other side of the street. He was holding a camera up to his face, pointing it at Vinnie. There were other cameras hanging from his neck.

"Don't look at me!" the man yelled – he sounded American. "It's all about angles and sunlight! Ask your art teacher in the morning!"

Vinnie's art teacher was Brother McConkey. He was probably the oldest man in the world, and the most savage. Vinnie's
da had told him that Brother McConkey had lived during the
Great Famine of 1845 to 1851. Not only that, he'd *caused*
the Great Famine by eating every cow, sheep, pig, and Mars
bar in the country, and he'd left nothing for anyone else. Art
classes went like this: Brother McConkey drew something on
the blackboard, and then you drew it on paper, exactly as it
was on the board; if it wasn't exact enough, Brother McConkey
took chunks out of you with a huge wooden ruler. Vinnie
wasn't going to ask Brother McConkey anything in the morning. Anyway, they were in the middle of the summer holidays.
They wouldn't be seeing Brother McConkey for another six
weeks – if he lived. Brother McConkey nearly died at least
three times a year.

They kept running. When they got to the end of the railings and Gertie had stopped chasing them, they came back
and crossed the street to meet the man with the cameras.

He was wearing one of those army camouflage jackets,
and trousers that had lots of pockets up the sides. And big
boots that might have been black once. And he had a ponytail, a grey ponytail. They'd never seen a man with a ponytail
before.

He was putting film into one of his cameras.

"Will we be in the paper, mister?" said Frankie.

"Magazine," said the man. "Maybe." ·

He was definitely American.

"What magazine?"

"*Newsweek*," said the man. "Heard of it?"

"No," they lied.

The man grinned. He wasn't young, but his grin was. It was a young fella's smile, on a face that was older than Vinnie's da's. It was the kind of smile that got you into trouble.

"You guys going to show me the sights?"

"Will you pay us?"

He laughed.

"Here," he said.

He was holding out a white handkerchief, for the cut on Frankie's lip.

"Thanks."

"Sure. Come on."

He wanted them to show him around, but he led the way, through Summerhill, into town. He asked them their names. And he told them his – George Keane.

"I'm more often called Gee."

"Why?"

"G is for George. So, Gee."

"That's thick," said Frankie.

"You don't like it?"

"It's stupid," said Frankie. "That would make me F."

He pointed at Vinnie.

"And Vinnie'd be V. It's thick."

"So," said the man. "Call me George. So, what are you guys going to show me today?"

"Do you want to see Nelson's Pillar?" said Vinnie.

"Sure."

"That's a pity," said Vinnie. "The IRA blew it up in 1966."

"Good one, Vee," said Frankie.

"Thanks, Eff," said Vinnie.

It didn't really matter where they brought George because he took photographs of everything. He held a camera in each hand, like a cowboy with his guns. He got down on his knees, so he could see under a passing lorry. He climbed up on the roof of a car, so he could look over the canal bridge wall. He never stopped.

"Were you in the war, George?" said Frankie.

"Well," said George. "Which war?"

"Any war."

"Well, then," said George. "I've seen a few."

"Like?"

"Vietnam."

"Really?" said Frankie. "He's spoofin'," he told Vinnie.

"Biafra," said George. "Israel. The Congo. Korea. Right back to good old W. W. Two."

"Germany?"

"The Pacific," said George. "Guadalcanal, Saipan, Japan."

"What are you doing here then?" said Vinnie. "There's no war here."

"What about the North?" said Frankie.

"That's not a war," said Vinnie. "That's just messing."

"It is so a war," said Frankie. "There's bombs and everything," he told George. "The British are up there and they've no right to be and my da says if they ever come down here they won't know what hit them."

"Your da will have to get up off his arse," said Vinnie.

"It would take more than the British army to make my da get up off his arse," said Frankie.

The holidays were often boring, even though they were always much better than school. Vinnie hated school, every brick and every minute. He couldn't wait for his next birthday, when he'd be fifteen and he could leave school. He was going to be a carpenter, like his da – only better. He'd walk out through the gates of the school and never look back at the dump. No more maths, no more Irish, English, history, geography, commerce, religion, civics, science, French, or art. Brother McConkey, RIP. But the holidays got boring too, when they got a bit sick of just hanging around and dossing, and there was nothing to do that didn't cost money or get them into trouble.

So meeting George Keane was great. They hung around with him for the next three days. He was good fun, for an old lad. And he was full of great stories. About invasions and escapes, and booby traps, and air raids, and jungles – and boxing.

"Ah," said Vinnie. "So, that's why you're here."

"Yes."

The big fight was coming up. The world's greatest boxer, Muhammad Ali, was in Dublin.

THE BIG FIGHT
Croke Park, Dublin
Muhammad Ali vs. Al "Blue" Lewis
July 19th 1972
Gates Open 6 p.m.
Main Event 8.45 p.m.

Vinnie knew the details off by heart. The posters were everywhere. Croke Park was the biggest stadium in Ireland. It was where the All-Ireland football and hurling finals were played every year, and the streets around Croke Park were full of country people who'd come up to Dublin for the day. Vinnie's house was beside Croke Park, right under one of the stands.

"If that stand ever falls on us," said Vinnie's da once, "we'll be crushed by a hundred tons of rubble and about two hundred tons of culchies."

This was at their dinner, just after a security man from Croke Park had knocked on the door to complain, because Vinnie had written "Welcome to Culchie Heaven" with black paint on one of the stadium's exit gates.

"Culchie" was the Dubliners' name for country people.

"Ah, God love them," said Vinnie's ma. "They have a hard life."

"The culchies?" said Vinnie's da. "What's hard about their lives?"

"All that fresh air," said his ma. "It must nearly kill them."

Vinnie lived right under the stand but he'd never been to

a Gaelic football or hurling match in Croke Park. His teachers, the Christian Brothers, loved Gaelic games. So Vinnie hated them. He'd never been to a match, but he went into Croke Park all the time, over the wall and wire, when it was shut and nobody was supposed to be there. There were little bits of Vinnie's trousers hanging from the barbed wire all around the stadium wall.

And that, in a way, was why George Keane ended up meeting Vinnie's granny, and Vinnie ended up meeting Muhammad Ali.

It happened this way: Vinnie and Frankie had brought George to Poolbeg Lighthouse, at the end of the South Wall. The Wall stretched out into Dublin Bay. The tide was high, and the wind was mad. They were getting drenched, although it wasn't raining, and once or twice Vinnie thought they were going to get blown into the sea. And it was getting late. The sun was going down behind them. It must have been nine o'clock.

George was right at the edge of the wall, taking pictures two at a time. He spoke into the wind, telling them a story, as if they were all at home beside the fire.

"I'll tell you, guys, the bullets were chopping the water around us, like water boiling in a pot waiting for pasta. Man, I still don't know how I didn't get hit. And, then –"

He swapped cameras. The Liverpool ferry was going past them, about ten feet from their noses.

"– And, then, we were on top of the barbed wire. Didn't see it. It was under the water, before we could get to the beach. Felt it bite before I knew what it was. I fell right into it."

"Did you get through it?"

"Well, I'm here."

"Smart-arse," said Frankie.

"Hey, George," said Vinnie. "I know some barbed wire I bet you couldn't get through."

They saw George get a bit angry. But not for long, a few seconds.

"What wire?" he said.

It was as if Vinnie had told George that he was lying, that his war stories were all made up – that was what George's voice sounded like to Vinnie. But Vinnie hadn't meant that at all. He'd believed George. It was just, when George mentioned barbed wire it had reminded Vinnie of the barbed wire on top of the wall around –

"Croke Park," said Vinnie.

"Where Ali's fighting," said George.

"Yeah."

"Come on," said George.

For the first time since they'd met him, he put down his cameras.

They followed him, all the way to Croke Park. It was dark now, and a bit cold. Vinnie should have been at home. He was in trouble, whatever happened.

They stood at the Canal End of the stadium. George looked up at the wall and the wire.

"Piece of cake," he said.

"This is mad," said Frankie.

"The great ideas are always mad," said George. "So, Vinnie," he said. "Let's see who can get over that wire up there."

Vinnie and Frankie looked at each other.

"Now?" said Vinnie.

It was a stupid question, because George was already climbing the wall. He was quick, and agile. It was mad, because he must have been more than fifty years old – they'd worked it out. And that was what made Vinnie and Frankie jump up on the wall and follow him. They had to prove that they were quicker, and more agile. They were forty years younger; this was their home. They couldn't let a middle-aged Yank get over the wire before them. Ireland vs. the USA. Youth vs. Old Age.

They all reached the wire at the same time.

A cop car went past, on Jones's Road. They were well away from its light, but it was still a bad moment. A good–bad moment, one of those ones. They started laughing. The car was gone, and they stood up on the wall.

Frankie went first. He gripped the stanchion that held the three rows of wire in place, and he put one foot over the wire. It was the bad part. He was very exposed. Anyone passing could see him. And he was stepping into darkness. The glow from the streetlights didn't make it to the other side of the wall. Both feet were over now. They heard him jump, and land. Vinnie followed; he couldn't wait. He felt the top wire pull at his trousers. But nothing ripped. He jumped.

He landed on the top terrace. On match day it would have

been packed, but now was just a low step. It wasn't a bad drop. He landed, and let himself roll.

George landed right beside him. A camera hit Vinnie's head. Lights flashed – he thought he was unconscious. But he knew: Either he was or he wasn't – he couldn't think he was. So he wasn't unconscious. But his head was very sore. And he was bleeding. And he must have roared or something, because Frankie's hand went over Vinnie's mouth, and Frankie was hissing at him to shut up. And there were lights all over and around them, and then one big light.

They'd been caught. They were surrounded by security men.

The whole stadium was like a building site. There was a half-built boxing ring in the centre of the pitch. There were piles of wood and scaffolding. There were huge sheets of canvas. There were hundreds of men around them; it seemed like hundreds. At least ten.

"I know these two," said a voice.

Light hit Vinnie's face. He held up his hands to block it.

"Will I call the Guards?" said another voice.

Vinnie couldn't really see the security men; the light was too strong.

"The cops," Frankie whispered to George, explaining who the Guards were.

"Who's this one?"

The light went to George's face. He looked straight into it.

"We don't know him," said Vinnie.

He was bleeding badly, his head was hopping – agony,

agony, agony – but he was suddenly delighted. It was a brilliant idea, pretending not to know George. It would save George, and maybe Vinnie and Frankie too. It was up to George.

George held up his press card.

"I followed you guys up here," he told the security men.

"Who are you?" said a security man.

Vinnie could see him now. It was the same guy who'd knocked at his door, to complain about Vinnie's painted message on the exit gate.

"Name's on the card," said George.

"Where did *you* come from?"

"Say," said George. "This kid is bleeding badly."

Vinnie heard George's camera click. There was no flash. Vinnie hoped the security men wouldn't notice.

He groaned.

"Which one of you guys hit him?" said George.

"None of us," said the security man.

"He'll need stitches," said George.

Vinnie groaned.

"Where's the nearest hospital?" said George.

Vinnie groaned.

"I'll take him," said George.

Vinnie groaned.

"Eh," said the security man. "OK."

Vinnie groaned, although he wanted to whoop.

"What about this one?" said another security man.

He was holding Frankie's arm.

"I'll need him," said George. "In case this guy's concussed and doesn't know who he is."

"Who am I?" said Vinnie, and regretted it. It was too much, way over the top. He groaned.

"Let's go," said George.

They started down the terrace. The security men got out of their way. George was impressive – the cameras, the army jacket, the accent, his age. There was no way they were going to grab him.

George stopped. Vinnie and Frankie stopped. They were going nowhere without George.

"Say, fellers," said George.

He was talking to the security men.

"Would you watch this for me?"

He held out one of the cameras.

"Look after this?"

It was a good touch. *You can trust me, lads. I'll be back for the camera.*

One of the security men took the camera. He held it like one of his future grandchildren.

"Thanks," said George.

"How will you get the camera back?" said Frankie when they were out the exit gate, on the street.

"It's broken," said George. "Beyond repair. It must be. It hit Vinnie's head."

George stopped a taxi and they went to the Mater Hospital. Vinnie had never been in a taxi before. It was only a car, really, but his da didn't have a car, so it was good, even though he was going for stitches and he knew he was in for more pain. And then he had to confront his ma and da. And his granny.

And his granny was the real point of the story. Even with Ali, Vinnie's stitches, and all the rest of it, his granny was the best part of it.

He went home, stitched. It was five in the morning. George came with him. And Frankie. Because Frankie was too scared to go home and face his parents.

Vinnie knocked on the door. His da opened the door. He heard his ma.

"Is that Vincent? Oh, thank God."

He suddenly knew what they must have been going through, all night, worried sick about him. He expected his da to roar at him, maybe even whack him. But his da was looking at him like he was delighted. Vinnie tried hard not to cry.

"Is that our Vincent out there?"

That was his granny. She came to the door. She shoved his da out of the way. She was able to do this without being rude; it was the way she moved, side to side, like a human duck. She grabbed Vinnie and dragged him into the hall.

"Aren't you the maggot?" she said.

She was talking to Vinnie – he thought she was – but she was looking at George.

"I'm sorry," said George.

He sounded like a kid.

"And who's that hiding?" said Vinnie's granny. "Is that Francis?"

Frankie hated his name.

"Howyeh, Mrs Fitzpatrick."

She was Vinnie's ma's ma.

"Come in, the lot of yis."

His granny took over the house when she visited.

They followed her into the hall, to the kitchen.

She wasn't all that old, but she made it seem like she'd been around since Ireland was invented. She muttered bits of Irish, and everything she wore was black, including her teeth. She'd been mourning Vinnie's grandad since 1957, two years before he actually died.

"She stared at him till his heart couldn't take any more."

"Stop that," said his ma. "He had a hard life."

"That's true," said his da.

She predicted things that often came true. They'd all been listening to the radio a few months before, and Elvis Presley was on. Vinnie's granny sat up and she pointed at the radio.

"That fella will die in 1977," she'd said.

"Elvis is the King," said Vinnie's da. "He'll live for ever."

But Vinnie had believed her.

Now, she was staring at George.

"You're not a happy camper," she said. "Are you, George?"

"You know my name," said George.

"That's nothing," said Vinnie. "She's only starting."

"Don't listen to that scut," said his granny. "Tell me all about it."

And that was what happened. George did what Vinnie's granny told him. His da brought Frankie home; he lived around the corner. And the rest of them had tea. It was daylight out by now; it was very early morning.

George talked. He sat in front of the granny and he talked and talked, for ages. He was tired of war: he'd seen terrible things – he'd done terrible things. He was tired of his life. He didn't know what he should do. Vinnie's da came back, but George kept talking. He was afraid of settled life, he said. He had a young daughter he hardly knew, and a wife he'd never really let himself know. He didn't know where his life was going.

"And that's why you've come to Ireland," said Vinnie's granny.

It was the first thing she'd said in thirty-seven minutes. George had been talking all that time.

"Isn't it, George?"

George nodded.

"Yes," he said.

"With your surname under your arm," said the granny. "George *Keane*. You've come looking for your roots."

He didn't nod this time.

"I'm not sure," he said.

"Good man," said the granny. "They'd be no bloody good to you. Even if you did find them. You'd only be codding yourself

120

if you thought your roots really mattered. It's the future that matters now. Not the past."

Vinnie was a bit stunned. His granny had never spoken like this before.

"Amn't I right, George?" she said.

"Yes," said George. "I guess so."

"Good man," she said. "He guesses so."

She leaned out and patted his leg.

"It'll be grand," she said. "Go home."

She patted his leg again.

"Give that daughter of yours her roots."

"I think it's too late," said George.

"Why is it?"

"I'm like a stranger to her."

"Go home and you won't be," said the granny. "It'll take a while. But listen here. Are you listening now, George Keane?"

They all waited. This was the bit they always loved, when she closed her eyes and did her predicting.

She closed her eyes.

"That girl will have two children. Two fine grandchildren for you, George. A boy, and a grand girl. Her name will be Margaret."

"That's your name, Granny," said Vinnie.

She opened her eyes.

"I know my own name, you maggot. And George. The boy will be called Jason. And, George, they'll be fine children and they'll do you proud."

She opened her eyes.

"Off with you now, George. You've a busy day tomorrow."

She looked at the light coming through the kitchen window.

"Today," she corrected herself. "You've to take your snaps of Muhammad Ali and you'll have to be quick to catch that fine man."

George stood up. He looked down at Vinnie's granny.

"Thank you," he said.

He went to the door. And stopped.

"Do I have family here? Keanes?"

"None worth knowing," she said. "But I'll tell you this now, George. There will be a Keane, called Roy. A great, great footballer. You were in Saipan before, George, I'm thinking."

"Yes," said George. "In 1945."

"Well, go back in 2002. And bring your camera."

George looked at Vinnie. He looked like he couldn't make his mind up; he wanted to hear more. He was stunned, excited.

He snapped out of it.

"I'll see you later," he said to Vinnie.

And he was gone.

The granny whacked Vinnie's knee.

"The bed for you, sonny."

"How do you do it?" said Vinnie.

"Do what?" she said.

"How did you know his name?"

"I heard you talking about him with the Francis fella."

"Then how about him looking for his roots?"

"Ah sure, all the Yanks are looking for their roots. That was easy."

"What about the grandchildren?"

"Ah sure now, he'll have forgotten all about me by the time he has grandchildren."

"Margaret?" said Vinnie.

"A grand name."

"And Jason?"

"It's a Yank kind of a name. Isn't there a fella called Jason in *Scooby-Doo*?"

"No."

"Ah well."

And that night George took Vinnie and Frankie to the fight. Their mas made them wear their Sunday clothes. George wore Vinnie's da's suit and he cut off his ponytail so the security men wouldn't recognize them.

It wasn't a great fight. They'd seen much better on the telly. But it was great to be there, right up near the ring – they could see the boxers' sweat, they could hear the men in their corners, shouting instructions. They could see the whole business.

And Ali won.

And after the fight, George brought them to Ali's dressing room. Down a tunnel, past big men in tight suits – they kept expecting to be stopped. But it didn't happen. They came to a door. George knocked. The door opened. George entered. They followed him.

It was hot in there, and crowded. Two or three big men got out of the way, and they could see Ali. He was sitting on the edge of a table. He was covered in towels. His head was down. He looked very tired.

He looked up and saw George. He sat up. He smiled.

"Gee," he said.

"Champ," said George.

And they met Ali.

Vincent punched him. So did Frankie. Ali showed them a few moves. And, just before he took them away, George took a photograph from his pocket. It was of Ali, fighting.

"Say, Champ," he said. "Will you sign this one for me?"

Ali took the photo.

"Will you sign it for my grandson?" said George. "Jason."

Ali signed the photograph.

"Did you ever meet George again, Da?"

"No," said Vincent. "No, I didn't."

He'd often thought about George. Every time he saw a picture of Ali, every time he saw a man with a ponytail, he thought about George. And he always wondered if he'd ever had a grandson called Jason or a granddaughter called Margaret.

Then, the year before the Special Olympics, in 2002, Vincent and Valerie, his wife, were watching the news. They watched Roy Keane, Ireland's greatest footballer, leaving Saipan, where the Irish team had gone to prepare for the World Cup. Keane was going home. He'd been thrown off the team; he was refusing to play. No one was sure what had happened.

Vincent started crying.

"Ah, for God's sake, Vincent," said Valerie. "It's only football."

"It's not," said Vincent. "It's my granny."

He wondered if George Keane was still alive and if he was in Saipan, taking pictures of Roy Keane. He'd have been very old by then, well into his eighties. He looked for George on the television. For days he looked, as the story got bigger and madder, but he didn't see George. But, as he looked at the news about Roy Keane and Saipan, he knew that, yes, his granny had been right. George had had his grandchildren. They were out there somewhere. And he wondered if he'd ever meet them.

And now, in 2003, as they all watched Nelson Mandela opening the Games in Croke Park, Vincent's daughter, Ciara, touched the scar on his forehead again.

"And you got that mark when George's camera hit you," she said.

"That's right," said Vincent.

"It's nice," she said. "It's not ugly."

"Like the rest of him," said Gavin.

And Vincent laughed.

"Don't listen to that scut," he said.

And he hugged his children.

Chapter 7
MIN

Behind Min's apartment there was a wild place. She liked to look out over the trees and rough meadows and swampland from her window on the twelfth floor. Sometimes there were deer, sometimes vultures, circling above some dead thing she couldn't see.

For two days in a row now there had been these odd flashes of light from a dense grove of cedar at the bottom of a steep escarpment. There seemed no pattern to the flashes – it wasn't code. At least, she didn't think it was.

"Is that where it came from?"

It was her mother. She tended to sneak up a lot these days.

"The dog, Jasmine. Do you think it's still out there?"

Min turned her attention back to the wild place – back to the glimmering in the dense tangle of green.

"The county should do something," said her mother. "Who knows what goes on out there?"

The light flashed again, but her mother didn't seem to notice. *It's only in my head,* thought Min. *Or someone trying to reach me.*

Her mother massaged Min's shoulders until she shrugged her off. Still, the woman wouldn't leave. Min could feel the weight of her waiting.

Then she kissed the back of Min's head. "Dinner in five, sweetie," she said, and tiptoed away as if leaving a hospital room.

"What kind of dog?" her father demanded the day it happened. The day of the attack.

"Honey, she's frightened enough. No need to shout."

"Sorry, Min." He sat on the sofa beside her, taking her hands in his as if she were six. "Did you catch the licence plate number?"

She dredged up a smile.

"Was it a schnauzer?" he asked. "I hate schnauzers. My uncle Bernie had one."

She withdrew her hands from his. Tucked them in her armpits.

"Don't know," she said, and hated the sound of her own voice.

"A Dobermann? One of those ugly – what do you call 'em? – Rottweilers. Was it a Rottweiler?"

She shook her head. "Grey," she said, just for something to say.

"The dog was grey?"

"Big," she said, as if she were a tourist in her own living room with a vocabulary borrowed from a phrase book.

Her mother stirred honey into Tension Tamer tea.

"Great Danes are grey," said her father. "God, they're huge! But it didn't bite you?"

She shook her head.

"A few scratches," said her mother. "Tore her shirt."

"Poor love," said her dad.

"Just scared me," said Min. "Scared me."

Then her mother held her close and talked over her head. "Cornered her, I guess. Maybe we could check with the pound?"

"Good idea," said her father, glad to have something to do. "There may have been other complaints. Maybe someone reported it missing."

He went off to call, and her mother rocked her like a little girl. But she wasn't a little girl. She was sixteen.

"Talk to me, honey," cooed her mother. "Whenever you're ready."

And six weeks later, she still wasn't ready.

Chloe had been all Oh-my-God about it, at first, and wanted to know everything – everything! But Min didn't want to talk. She could cobble together a story inside her head, but a story was just for someone who wanted attention. Min did *not* want attention.

"OK," said Chloe. "So let's talk about something else. How about Mark Sedakis, for starters."

"Ummm, tasty," said one of the others. "And who do we

want for the main course?" And they were off.

Min listened and smiled on cue, so that no one really noticed she was slipping away. No one but Chloe, who brought her expensive bath salts the next day and said, "Soak it out, girl."

The bath salts were long gone and so was Chloe. "We're here for you, Jazz. We're trying. But you need help."

What Min needed, as far as she was concerned, was to be invisible. If she'd been invisible this would never have happened. If she'd never talked to the dog in the first place. Made nice – let it lick her hand.

Being invisible didn't take much. The trick was that you couldn't actually *not* show up. If you went missing, people came looking for you. So you filled your seat in class each day, handed every assignment in on time, answered only the questions you were asked, and otherwise faded into the background. Someone cracks a joke – you don't laugh. Someone needs help – you don't help. You don't give yourself away.

There was a path into the wild place beyond the rubbish bins at the foot of the apartment parking lot. Min followed the path down into the cool, green light, then veered off on a deer path, trusting the compass in her head. She came, at last, to a bluff just above the cedar grove, and there was the source of the mysterious brightness. A huge heap of glass. It was as if someone had taken a sledgehammer to a glass castle. But glass castles were the stuff of fairy tales. She gazed up to the top of the escarpment. More likely some unscrupulous wrecker had dumped the whole mess some dark and stormy night.

Then she saw the boy. He had a camera. He didn't notice her, standing on the rise looking down on him. She crouched and watched him silently.

He was about her age, she guessed, and his camera was odd – boxy and old-fashioned. He looked down into the view-finder rather than holding it to his eye. He was trying different angles – on his knees, flat on his stomach, perched on a nearby boulder. He was completely entranced. Min dared to come silently down off her hill, unafraid, invisible.

The sun came and went behind the clouds so that the broken castle of glass was sometimes dazzling and other times filled with sharp-edged shadows and off-kilter reflections. A glistening iceberg.

The boy took it all in, only stopping to switch lenses.

Click and *click* and *click.*

He didn't see her, or so she thought. But when she turned to leave, he called.

"What do you think it was?" he said.

She turned, halfway up the hill, and shrugged.

"I'm thinking the Hubble Telescope," he said. "Blown off course in a solar storm, or whatever."

She shrugged again.

"Then again, it could be a UFO," he said. "Or I guess you'd have to call it a UCLO – an unidentified crash-landing object?"

His hair was semisweet-chocolate streaked with cinnamon. His eyes were almond-shaped as if maybe there was Asian in him, though his irises were blue as sky. *Who knows where people come from any more*, she thought. *Mars?* And the thought made her smile, a no-no for the invisible.

"Jason," he said, waving. "And yes, I know, I talk too much."

She waved back, a little sock-puppet kind of wave.

He looked at the heap of glass, his hands on his hips. "It's gorgeous, isn't it? A gorgeous wreck. Not exactly environmentally friendly, but still. . ."

He glanced back up the hill toward her, and right then the sun turned the glass heap into an inferno, and Jason, backlit, was reduced to a silhouette. It freaked her out a bit and she turned to go.

"Hey," he shouted. "I just remembered where we met."

She turned again, frowned, and stuck her hands deep into the pockets of her jacket, as if she might be able to escape down the twin bolt-holes she had dug there.

"You were with Chloe and Sarah and that crew at Brendan's Pizza. Remember?"

She shook her head. She remembered the pizza parlour, all right. It had been months ago, Chloe's birthday. But the boy. . .?

"I was the leprechaun who served you," he said. "Maybe you don't recognize me without a plastic slice of pizza on my head."

Now she remembered him.

"Top o' the mornin'," he said, grinning cheekily, and danced a jig, holding the camera away from his body with one hand.

"You were great," he said. "Took a bite out of my hat – or threatened to, anyway. Oh yeah, and you actually sang the awful birthday song with me in harmony. That was you, right?" She nodded. "Which might suggest you have absolutely no musical taste, *or* that you are just a really, really good sport."

The compliments were piling up around her feet thick as molasses. If she didn't move soon, she'd be stuck.

She did her sock-puppet wave, and headed back up the hill. She had seen a rattletrap ten-speed bike leaning against a rock. He wouldn't follow her, not the path she was taking.

She didn't think he went to her school. She looked out for him the next day, a little bit anxious, a little bit eager. But no, she was safe, after all.

Then, three days later, he showed up at the apartment.

"There's a boy here to see you," said her mother, poking her head into Min's bedroom. The look on her mother's face said that if this boy could slay the dragon, they'd probably give him her hand in marriage and half the kingdom.

Jason stood by the picture window in the living room looking out at the wild place. He turned when she entered and it was as if there was a piece of the glass castle glinting in his blue eyes. Neither of them spoke until Min's mother got the hint and left the room.

"So," he said. "I tracked you down."

She waited.

"You can blame Chloe," he said. "I called her up and asked who her talkative friend was."

Min sagged against the wall, examined the carpet.

"Sorry," he said. "That was totally rude. I just came to give you something."

He held out a large, white envelope. She hesitated. Then took it from him. Inside was a photograph, an eight-by-ten, of the gorgeous heap of broken glass. It was brilliantly in focus, an angular collage full of bright splinters of sky and sharp wedges of earth, cropped so tightly that there was no sense of depth or scale. An Abstract Expressionist painting.

"Wow," she said.

"Look closer."

She looked closer and gasped. There she was – her image, anyway – reflected in a jagged shard.

"And you thought I didn't know you were there," he said. His grin was a tractor beam; she stepped back out of its force field.

"It's great," she said, holding out the photo to him.

He took it and looked it over with pride. "It is, isn't it. I mean, it's the best thing I've done so far. I'm just learning." Then he held it out to her again. "It's yours if you want it."

So she took it, wondering how long they could play pass-the-photo. She sat down with a coffee table between them. She felt like Icarus. She didn't want to get too close and run the risk of her wax melting.

133

He sat with the picture window behind him, backlit again in the late afternoon sun, featureless. Maybe he really was an alien. Maybe the heap of glass was his shattered starship.

"The camera belonged to my grandfather," he said. "He was this famous photographer, travelled the world. I found the camera in his stuff. Thought I'd take it out for a spin."

He chuckled as if she'd made some witty remark – as if they were having a conversation.

"I doubt I'm ever going to make a living at it, but I'm hooked. I'm taking a course up at the college."

She nodded, and he nodded, and fearing the nodding might get out of control, she looked at the picture again. This distorted blonde girl growing out her fringe in a heap of broken glass. Trapped as if by a curse.

"Well," he said, getting to his feet. "I've taken up a lot of your time."

She led him to the front door.

"Thanks, Jason," she said.

"Keane," he said.

"Yeah, I guess. . ."

"No, it's my name. Jason Keane."

She felt like a fool. She opened the door, but he didn't seem in any hurry to leave.

"Chloe told me about the dog incident," he said.

She leaned against the closet door, wrapped her arms around her chest and waited for the questions she wouldn't answer. He waited too, but she could outwait anyone, even this cocksure charmer with the good eye and the bad bike and no sense of boundaries.

"OK, I'll level with you," he said. "I'm Jason Keane Henschler, but I'm dropping the Henschler as soon as it's polite. For professional reasons. Assuming I ever have a profession. Keane was my grandfather's name."

She tried glaring, unsuccessfully.

"I got really screwed up when he died," he said. "Well, it was other stuff too. Got myself in big trouble." She stared at him, tense now, wondering where this was going. "I felt something had been stolen from me, you know? Not just my grandfather but – oh, Christ. Listen to me. Sorry."

Their eyes met and it was like bumper cars. But it was only Min who got knocked off course.

"Hey, we make a good couple," said Jason. "I mean I'm this motormouth who can't shut up, and you're –"

"Stalled?"

He looked pained at the gaffe he had made. Good. He deserved it. And before he could get his motormouth back in gear, she closed the door on him.

She leaned against it, felt the heat drain from her cheek into the cold wood. And then the dog was there with her in the narrow hallway. She smelled the meat on its teeth. She pressed her eyes shut, pressed her body against the door. Felt the dog's cold nose bury itself in her palm.

"Leave me alone," she said. "Please, just leave me alone."

*   *   *

Jason was leaning against the door too. Silently banging his head against it, actually.

"Leave me alone," he heard her say. "Please, just leave me alone."

It was more or less what he'd said, after Gee died. *Scram, everyone! Better still, I'll scram.* But no one seemed to get the message. They hung in. Wouldn't let him go. Thank God.

"No way," he whispered to the door.

And sure enough, he showed up at Min's school a few days later. He hung out on Waterloo Street, perched on his bike, leaning against the fence that marked the eastern boundary of the campus, guessing the way she'd go home. For three days he showed up and missed her every time, until finally he caught a glimpse of her way off, heading south, unaccountably, down Hillside. He raced to catch her, passing her on the hill, skidded to a squeaky and less than elegant stop by the kerb.

She was plugged into her iPod. She stopped, frowned from under her fringe.

"Who you listening to?" he asked.

She paused to give him time to reconsider – to just plain give up. But he wouldn't. So, she handed him the earphone.

"Ani diFranco," he said, nodding approvingly. "Does she sing your pain?"

Shit. He'd done it again. But to his surprise, she nodded. Mercifully – *unbelievably* – she had missed the irony in his voice. She even pushed the pause button. Progress.

"You?" she said. And he took it to mean what did he listen to.

"David Gray, Damien Rice, this freaky Icelandic band Sigur Rós."

"Sad music?"

"Yeah," he nodded enthusiastically. "Hey, I'm not *just* an annoying, chatty person. I've also got this annoying, melancholy, Irish thing going."

He watched Jasmine consider what he had said, almost saw some kind of a response form in her eyes. Then she turned on the music again in her head and he could see Ani start pumping through her veins. All that vitality Jasmine didn't seem to have herself. And yet. . .

"I wanted to talk to you about a project," he said. She frowned. Pushed the pause button again.

"Jason—"

"I want to do a series of photographs of you. It's for a school project."

"Don't do this—"

"At least listen to the idea, OK?"

Reluctantly, she took off her earphone, shoved it down into her coat pocket. They were at the bottom of the hill by now. She walked and he cruised at a snail's pace beside her, always one wheel rotation away from falling over.

He wanted to do a series of photographs of her carrying a pane of broken glass around with her for one whole day.

She stopped, stared at him, her mouth open in disbelief.

"You know, in class, at the dinner table, the bathroom – whatever. Well, not the bathroom but, you know – one whole day. This totally pretty girl just going through her day, ho-hum, except she's lugging around this big, sharp, scary piece of glass wherever she goes."

He could see her puzzlement drift pretty quickly toward exasperation.

"I got the idea from the picture of you in the glass," he said. "You know, the one I brought—"

She nodded, impatiently. "I figured that much."

"So?"

"So, why?"

"It seemed cool. No. No, that's not what I mean. It seemed *right*."

She didn't look one bit grateful for all his attention. As far as he could tell, she hadn't even picked up on the "totally pretty girl" reference.

"It's like a metaphor," he said.

"I get it!" she snapped.

Which is when he fell off his bike.

She broke up. The laughter burst out of her like water from an untangled hose. Then she covered her mouth, regained her composure. She stared at him sadly and shook her head.

"Nice try," she said, and left.

Jason scrambled to his feet and, dragging his wretched bike, ran to catch up. "OK, I'm sorry, but let me explain, Min, please."

She didn't hit him. He took that as a good sign.

"My grandpa, Gee – that's what we called him – didn't travel the world taking pics for tourist magazines. He was this socially conscious kind of miracle. He had a nose for chaos, for disaster: Hiroshima, Bangladesh, Eritrea, Darfur – wherever the world was falling apart, he'd be there. You know what I mean?"

She glanced warily at him. "And?" He hadn't lost her, yet. He stumbled on.

"It wasn't exploitation he was after. He was like trying to make sense of these tragedies. His pictures are. . . Oh, beautiful and horrible, and they ask hard questions. It's like out of chaos he finds this shred of . . . I don't know what . . . order, humanity."

"What are you getting at?" she said.

His eyes lit up. "Yesterday, I went down to the glass heap. That's what I was going to do for my photo series for school, this still-life exploration, blah, blah, blah. And then, it was like Gee was with me. And he was saying, 'So is that all you've got to say, Jason? What about the girl, Jason? The one trapped inside the glass, Jason?'"

He stopped talking. He had gone way too far. He stared at the wheel of his bike. It was badly bent. But, to his surprise, she didn't leave. And when he had given her lots of time to come to her senses and realize what a complete idiot he was, she was still there and, at last, he dared to look up.

"OK," she said.

She agreed to meet him in the wild place the next day. She was late, on purpose, hoping he would give up on her. Then she ended up running to get there, arriving sweaty and breathless. She needn't have worried. He was sitting cross-legged on a rock, like a Buddha in ochre-coloured running shoes. A Buddha in a black tee, with a chunky old camera slung around his neck.

She chose a pane the size of a Monopoly board, with two jagged teeth at the top. He had brought some emery paper to sand down the edge so she wouldn't get any slivers. He had brought Windex and paper towels.

She hoisted the glass in one arm, the way she might carry a book. It was thick, as heavy as an atlas.

"How does it feel?"

"Weird."

"Yeah, well. . ."

He stepped back to take her picture. "Don't look at me," he said. And so she looked at the pile of broken glass. There was probably a shattered piece there for every unhappy kid in the city.

He photographed her all the way home through the dappled woods, talking a mile a minute. "So you get used to me," he said. "So I become invisible to you." And Min thought how strange it was the different ways people try to make themselves invisible.

They had to get permission for the shoot at the school. It took over a week. Throughout it all, Jason was as stubborn as he was smooth. There were safety factors to consider. The principal wanted letters of reference, an insurance waiver, a plan, a storyboard, demarcations, limitations.

Time and again Min was ready to bail, but something made her hang in. She felt as if she had been floating off in space somewhere in a vacuum and maybe it was time to come back. Re-entry was the hardest part of space travel, right? The most dangerous part. She couldn't do it alone. Maybe Jason could be her Houston.

Ms Booth didn't mind them interrupting chemistry. While Jason did the shoot, she lectured the class on glass – silicates and alkali fusing at high temperatures. Despite its hardness, its brittleness, she said, glass was liquid.

Min wrote in her notebook, studiously, while Jason kneeled on the floor beside her desk, shooting up at her face through the slab of glass she held in the crook of her arm.

He took another group of pictures at her locker, even

squeezed himself inside to get the shot he wanted of her opening the door.

He shot her in the cafeteria where she ate alone. He shot her drinking at a water fountain and in the crowd at an after-school basketball game among cheering schoolmates pumping the air with their fists, while Min sat perfectly still, her pane held tightly to her chest.

Then he snapped off a number of shots on the way home but he wasn't happy with them. It was dull, overcast. Anyway, they were both tired.

He shot her at the dining room table, eating with her parents. He shot her brushing her teeth, and reading *A Long Way Down* on her bed. Finally, by the tiny glow of a night-light, he shot her asleep – or pretending, anyway – the pane lying beside her, its jagged teeth resting on the pillow so near her pale face.

When they turned the lights back on, he noticed the picture he had given her, framed on her wall above her desk. And there was another surprise. A group picture of Min and Chloe and four other girlfriends, all squished together in a booth at Brendan's, holding gooey slices of pizza up for the camera.

"You took that," she said.

"You're right! Chloe had one of those disposable cameras." He examined the picture closely.

"It's pretty good," said Min.

He turned to her, smiling. "I wasn't admiring the picture."

At the door to the apartment he said, "Can we do the outside shots again tomorrow, if it brightens up?"

She closed her eyes, drained.

"You're exhausted," he said. "I'm sure I've got something I can use."

She sighed and shook her head. "Tomorrow's OK," she said.

They met again after school the next day. He handed her the sheet of glass, freshly cleaned, still smelling of Windex. She didn't look glad to see it. She hadn't slept so well. Bad dreams. Yesterday had been hard. She had gone from being invisible at school to certified freak. Sometimes you burned up on re-entry.

"It's almost over," he said, and she glared at him. Then they started down Hillside Drive.

"Wait," he said. "Why do you go this way?" He looked east along Waterloo. "I can see your place from here. It's like six or seven blocks."

She scowled and headed toward Hillside anyway.

"Jasmine," he said. "I don't get it."

"No," she said. "You don't." She embraced the glass in both arms, her chin framed in the cleft between the two wicked teeth. "I don't know why you think you should 'get it'. It's not yours to get, OK?"

He held up his hands in peace. "I hear you," he said. "But I have to work tonight. Early. If I'm late, Brendan will fire me."

She shrugged.

"You don't care if I get fired?" She rolled her eyes. "Jesus!"

"OK, OK!" she said. She gazed at the pane and he could see her reflection in it.

Click.

She glared at him again. Then they headed east along Waterloo.

They were only three blocks from her place when it happened. She started to slow down, finally coming to a dead stop outside a miniature bungalow with a postage-stamp lawn. A dog lay on the tiny, crooked veranda. A tawny-coloured dog the size of a loaf of bread – fluffy bread – its pointy snout resting on its paws, a rhinestone collar around its neck.

Min stood at the end of the pathway staring at the dog. It raised its head. A yellow leash was attached to the wrought iron railing.

"Min?"

She didn't seem to hear him. She just stared at the dog. It sat up now, its tail wagging. Company! And Min started to walk up the path.

"What is it, Jasmine?"

Now the tiny dog was on its feet wiggling with excitement, its tail wagging furiously. It barked, and Jasmine stopped halfway between the house and the sidewalk. The dog barked again, wanting her to come closer. It strained on its leash, yapping furiously. Yapping so much that the front door opened, finally, and a man appeared. An old man with saggy, yellow skin and tousled grey hair. He wore a stained white T-shirt and baggy twill trousers held up with suspenders.

"What is it, Pixie?" he said. Then he saw Min and smiled. "You can pet her if you like," he said. "She don't bite."

Click.

The noise of the shutter drew the man's attention to Jason. "What is this?" he said, narrowing his eyes.

Click.

The dog was yapping like crazy now, dancing around at the end of its leash. "Shhh now, girl," said the man. But his attention was all on Min.

Quickly, Jason changed lenses, in time to see in his viewfinder the dawn of recognition on the old man's face.

"What do you want?" he said to Min. "What's that boy think he's doing?"

Click.

Min walked toward the man like a zombie. He glanced nervously at the pane of glass in her hands and backed toward his door. "You get on with you," he shouted, grabbing the door handle. "You're scaring the dog."

Click.

Pixie looked anything but scared. She was leaping and writhing in mid-air with excitement as Min drew nearer and nearer, until, at last, she stood at the bottom of the three stairs that led up to where the old man cowered in his doorway.

Min raised the glass high above her head.

CLICK

Click.

The man covered his face.

Click.

She smashed the glass down on the stairs.

Click.

The dog cringing in the corner of the veranda, whimpering. The man shrieked, withdrawing into the darkness of his doorway. And like an animal set free from a cage, Min started howling at him, screaming blue bloody murder.

The noise brought the next-door neighbour out on to her porch. By then Jason was dragging Jasmine away down the path. The man was clutching his arm, which was bleeding.

"What the heck is going on?" said the neighbour. She was in a housecoat and slippers.

"Call the cops," said the old man.

"Yes!" screamed Jasmine, struggling to free herself from Jason's grasp. "Good idea."

The woman stared at Jasmine, the broken glass, her elderly neighbour now sitting on his doorstep dabbing at his forearm with a filthy handkerchief. Pixie bounced around his knees, yapping like mad.

"Maybe, I just better," said the neighbour.

She tramped back toward her house, and the old man called after her, "Bernice, I need help here."

"And you're going to get it," she said, slamming her front door behind her. By now, Jason had dragged Jasmine to the sidewalk, where she shook him off. She was breathing heavily – they both were – but she made no further attempt to go at the old guy. It was over.

"Come on," he said. "Quick."

But she kept staring at the man, and Jason had never seen such rage in all his life. Too much rage to capture on film. His grandpa's sturdy old camera surely would explode with so much anger trapped inside it.

There was a bench beside a bus stop a block along the street, where Jasmine finally collapsed. And while Jason held her, she told him through her tears of old man McGregor. Of seeing him one day on her way home from school, emptying his cart, struggling with his bad hip and his groceries up the steps to the little bungalow.

"Can I help you, sir?" she had said, because she knew him from trick-or-treating and selling Girl Scout cookies back when there was a Mrs McGregor.

She carried his groceries into his kitchen for him, Pixie dancing at her feet, tripping her up, a fluffy little whirlwind. And just as soon as Min had put the last bag on the table, she turned her attention to the affectionate pup, cupping its tiny face in her hands and patting its wriggling, little body, talking happy nonsense. "Good dog. Good Pixie. Oh, such a good dog."

Which is when McGregor grabbed her from behind, his arms stronger than she would have ever imagined, encircling her, his hands squeezing and pinching and shoving.

She cried and held on to Jason and he held on to her as gently as if she was, despite all appearances, something liquid and melting.

"If I'd just kept my mouth shut!" she shouted.

"It wasn't your fault."

"That stupid, stupid dog."

"It wasn't the dog's fault, either."

"My mouth *betrayed* me," she said.

In time the tears subsided, but she still kept her face buried in his shoulder. "I didn't want anyone to know. Didn't want anyone to see me."

He didn't speak, just worked steadily at lassoing her breathing, getting it in sync with his, then slowing it down, down. Reeling her gently back to shore.

Someone nearby cleared her throat. It was Bernice, the neighbour. She had thrown a ratty brown sweater on over her housecoat.

"Is he all right?" Min asked.

"He'll survive. What about you, dear?"

Min sniffed, nodded.

"He's a sick man," said Bernice. "Ever since June died. I've seen. . . Well, I've seen things." She bit her lip. "I should have called the authorities, but I needed proof, you see. If he . . . I mean, would you . . . can you. . ."

"Yes," said Jasmine. "Yes."

She gave Bernice her phone number. Then Jason walked her home. He was half an hour late for work, but he made up for it by staying late to help clean up. Brendan was impressed.

Min went to the opening of the student exhibition at the college, where she met Jason's parents, Frank and Gina, and his kid sister, Maggie, who took a shine to Min in a big way. Maggie didn't even realize it was Min in the pictures. She had got her hair cut by then, short and perky. Chloe's suggestion.

There were twelve pictures in the series, in two neat rows. The first one was the princess trapped in the glass castle. That's how Min described it to Maggie.

"Like a fairy tale," said Maggie, who stepped back to scan the wall. "Except there doesn't seem to be any prince."

"Oh, there's a prince," said Min, "and a wizard, except he only appeared to the prince in a kind of a vision."

"Humph," said Maggie, clearly disappointed. "So where is this prince?"

Min smiled to herself. Jason was talking a blue streak to someone. His professor, maybe. Or was it Brendan from the pizzeria? "Well," she said, "the prince was the one who wrote down the story, you see. The princess had to rescue herself. At least, she had to do all the grunt work."

Maggie rolled her eyes. "Oh, *that* kind of a fairy tale," she said.

"Yeah, sorry."

"And this old man, is he supposed to be the dragon or the

ogre or something? Because, for one thing, his dog is way too cute, and the man just looks kind of mangy and befuddled."

"Yeah," Min admitted. "A poor excuse for a dragon."

"Oh, well," said Maggie, sighing, and she scooted along to the last picture. "At least it ends happily."

Because the story didn't end on Mr McGregor's front step. Jason had gone back, by himself, to the wild place and reshot the photograph that had started the whole thing. But now, of course, there wasn't a girl trapped in the glass, any longer. Just a jagged piece of empty blue sky.

Chapter 8
JIRO

When my older brother came home from the war, he had no legs. He lost them in a place called Luzon, in the Philippines, where our Japanese soldiers were fighting the Americans. My brother, Taro, was advancing with his platoon through the jungle toward the enemy position, when the grenades started falling from the trees like big fat fruit. He said he didn't even know what hit him.

Luzon is in the tropics, Taro said. He had shipped out a week earlier, and everything was new to him and strange. He said it was so hot it felt like your skin was melting, like it would just fall from your bones. My brother liked the heat. He liked the cold too. He used to love walking and hiking in the mountains. He loved looking at plants and insects, and identifying them by their names. Back in Sapporo, where our family is from, he used to take me on long walks in the woods, or along the beach, and tell me all the names of everything we saw – the trees, the flowers, even the shells that washed up from the sea. And not just the Japanese names, either. He knew the names in English, and he knew the scientific names too. These were in Latin, which is a language so old that nobody even remembers how to speak it any more – and *that* shows you how smart my brother is. He wanted to be a scientist and study botany, which is the science of plants. He was studying this in university when they drafted him and sent him to war. Now he can't be a scientist. He can't take walks any more either.

He didn't tell me a whole lot about the day he lost his legs, but I know him pretty well, and I can picture it in my mind. He was probably marching along with the rest of his buddies, just waiting for the enemy to jump out from behind the thick curtains of leaves and start shooting at them. He was probably scared, at least at first, because Taro wasn't cut out to be a soldier, even though he was the oldest son. I'm the second, but I'm more of the soldierly type – crazy, fearless – at least that's what our mother said. Frankly, between you and me, Taro was kind of a sissy. I loved him like crazy, but he was more of a scholar or a teacher, with his round glasses and skinny wrists. He would have made a really great scientist.

But it's too late for that. There he was, scared out of his wits, following his platoon through the jungle. It was meltingly hot, and the damn fat tropical leaves kept smacking him in the face. Huge spiders dangled from vines in front of him, catching him up in their sticky webs. The insects were humming and screeching, and the jungle buzzed with life. And sooner or later, in spite of his fear, old Taro would have become interested, you know? He couldn't have helped it. He would have become interested because to him, the spiders and the fat-leaved plants were a hell of a lot more fascinating than killing people you hadn't even met yet.

I figure he started to lag behind a little, and maybe he even stopped to inspect a little snake dangling from a tree limb, or to study the underside of a leaf. And that's when the heavy fruits started dropping from the trees.

Plop! The grenade dropped on to the spongy jungle floor, and maybe it bounced a little, and then another dropped. They looked like miniature pineapples, but of course they weren't. Nor were they coming from the trees above. They came from way back, beyond the trees, where the Americans were hiding in ambush. Up ahead, Taro's sergeant was yelling, *Throw them back! Throw them all back!* but Taro couldn't hear very well because he had lagged too far behind. By the time he understood the sergeant's order and ran over to pick one up, it was too late. The pineapple exploded at his feet, and the last thing he recalls is his body being lifted up from the earth toward the jungle canopy and the sky beyond.

"What happened then?" I asked.

He shrugged and rubbed the place where his leg used to be. "Don't remember coming down again," he said.

The way I see it, that's a good thing.

Now, I should introduce myself properly. My name is Jiro, which means "second" in Japanese, because I was the second-born son. Taro is named Taro because he was the first. When Taro was drafted into the army and lost his legs, he was almost eighteen. It was 1944, and I had just turned nine at the time, but I was small for my age. My mother says it's because I didn't get enough rice to eat during the war, due to all the food shortages, but I didn't care. I was small, but I was scrappy, and I would have made a great soldier. Back then, I wanted nothing more than to be shipped off to Luzon in the Philippines to kill Americans, and when Taro was drafted, I thought I would drop dead from envy.

I would gladly have gone to fight in his place and left him to study his books so he could become a scientist. But the one thing you learn during war is that you can't pick and choose, and in the end, pretty much everyone is a loser. Some people lose their lives, others lose their families or their honour. My brother lost his legs. He was one of the lucky ones.

Taro, being almost ten years older than me, was always taller, but when he was shipped back from Luzon, he was shorter. We finally tracked him down in an army hospital out-side Tokyo. There were wounded soldiers everywhere, in the rooms, in the hallways. When we found the bed with his name on it, it was empty.

"He's dead!" our mother cried, throwing herself across the bare mattress and starting to weep.

I wanted to cry too, but just then I heard this rackety noise like a street vendor's cart, and I turned to see Taro. He was sitting on a wooden plank with wheels on it. He rolled himself awkwardly across the concrete floor and came to a halt at my feet.

"Well," he said, looking up at me. "Guess I can't call you 'Little Brother' any more."

Our father had been killed during a fire bombing, and Taro was the only family we had left. When we heard he was alive, my mother and I travelled all the way down from Sapporo to the hospital in Tokyo to find him. The trip was almost impossible back then because the tracks had been bombed, and many of the trains had stopped. There were curfews at night, and our Emperor had come on the radio to surrender, and we knew that the Americans were on their way. We were terrified of them, or rather my mother was. To tell the truth, I was too, although I took care not to show it. We learned in school that Americans were evil *oni*, long-nosed devils, who would hurt us in terrible ways, especially our women. So while we travelled, I was on the lookout for American devils, ready to protect my mother.

The first time I saw one up close was at a train station in Tokyo. He was as tall as a giant, with scary pale eyes and colourless hair and skin as pale as a mushroom. At first I thought he was a ghost. His mouth was stretched wide from side to side, baring his enormous teeth, which confused me because I never thought that ghosts had teeth. Then he started walking towards us, and I realized he couldn't be a ghost because in Japan our ghosts don't have legs.

If he wasn't a ghost, he must be an American.

I stood up tall and stepped bravely into his path, in front of my mother.

"*Damé!*" I cried. "Stop!"

The American stopped. He spoke some gibberish that I couldn't understand and held out his hand. In it was a bar wrapped in bright coloured paper, with English writing on it that I couldn't read.

"It's candy!" my mother said. "Jiro-chan, take it!"

I was hungrier than you can even imagine, but I knew better than to trust the food offered by an *oni*. I looked right into those evil blue eyes, curled my lip, and shook my head.

The American's mouth got small. He shrugged his shoulders. He unwrapped the bar and took a bite, humming and raising his bushy eyebrows, making a big show of how tasty it was. He held it out again, and I could see now that it was chocolate, and I could smell its delicious smell. My mouth started to water.

My mother stepped in front of me. She bowed deeply to the American and held out her hand. I could see her fingers trembling, she was so hungry.

Other big-nosed American soldiers were standing around. They started to laugh, like my mom was the funniest thing they'd ever seen. My face turned hot and red.

A group of children spotted us and came running.

"*Chodai! Chodai!*" they cried, jumping up and down. "*Pu-leee-zu*, candy!"

The American soldiers had lots of candy bars. They threw

them on the ground and made the children scramble. They tossed them further and further away, and made the children run. It was a game to them. The Japanese children, dressed in filthy rags, were pushing and shoving and snatching the bars from the dirt and from each other. The American soldiers in their clean, pressed uniforms were laughing.

"No!" I wanted to scream to the children. "Throw them all back!" But I knew it was no use. They were too hungry. We all were. I turned away and saw my mother peeling the wrapper off a small piece of chewing gum. It wasn't even food! I reached over and slapped her hand and knocked it to the ground. Wordlessly, my mother picked it up again and put it in her sleeve. There is no way to describe the shame I felt.

I didn't know it then, but that American soldier was Mr Gee. The next time I saw him was in the hospital ward, and I didn't recognize him as the soldier with the candy bar. He was with a group of American army doctors, and they were going from ward to ward, inspecting our injured Japanese people. Mr Gee had a camera, and he was taking pictures of the wounded.

They weren't interested in soldiers like Taro who had been wounded on the battlefield. They only wanted to examine the civilians, old men and young ladies and children, who had been sent up from Hiroshima and Nagasaki where they dropped the big bombs. Atom bombs. Bombs that made people's skin melt and fall from their bones. This is what the Americans wanted pictures of, and I hated them for that.

CLICK

It is hard to tell a foreigner's age just by looking, but I guessed that Mr Gee was younger than the doctors who were ordering him to take the pictures. He seemed nervous, being near all those wounded people. I think he felt sorry having to take their pictures. I could understand his feeling. I mean, we used to have a camera too, and we liked to take snapshots when we went on holiday. But we were not on a holiday, and who would want to remember this? It seemed to me better just to forget, and yet, I couldn't forget, nor could I forgive Mr Gee for taking those pictures.

I saw him again a couple of weeks later. Taro had been discharged, and he had joined up with a group of wounded veterans from the hospital, begging for alms on a street corner by the train station. He didn't want to be a beggar, but he didn't have much choice. Our mother had never recovered from the shock of seeing her eldest son with no legs, and she had fallen ill with a sickness of the nerves, caused by an excess of grief. I was still only ten, and too young to support a sick mother and a crippled brother. I did odd jobs when I could find them, but mostly I pushed Taro around on his plank to and from the station. At night we slept in a rooming house with the other wounded veterans, in a small dark room the size of a closet.

All of the vets in Taro's group were missing something – arms, or legs, or eyes, or ears – but somehow, together, they got along pretty well. The ones with legs carried the legless ones about. The ones with arms fed the armless. The ones with all their fingers played sad, old songs on an accordion. Luckily, all of them could sing. They wore the white robes of repentance over their ragged military uniforms, and they painted signs in large Japanese characters, saying how war was bad, and they were sorry they had fought and caused so much grief and suffering.

At first, people gave them money, but as the months passed and the war began to fade from memory, people began to ignore them. I watched from across the street.

"It's like you're all ghosts," I said. "Invisible. They walk right by you!"

"They're ashamed," Taro said.

At the end of the day, when I pushed my brother home over the pitted streets, he was so tired he had trouble hanging on to his plank. His injuries had weakened him. When we passed in front of a noodle stand, he motioned for me to stop.

"Wait," he said. He untied the corner of his shirt and handed me two coins, his share of the day's money. "I could sure use some noodles."

I bought a bowl and brought it back to him. The steam from the soup rose up and bathed my face, and the fat noodles glistened. I hadn't eaten all day, and I thought I would faint, I was so hungry. I handed the bowl to him. He sniffed the fragrant steam. "Mmm," he said. "Delicious." He inhaled again, then handed the bowl back to me. "You have the rest."

"But you didn't eat any!" I exclaimed.

"I don't need to," he said. "Ghosts get fat from smelling the steam."

When Mr Gee showed up, I recognized him by his camera. He was standing off to one side, watching the veterans sing and play the accordion. A little girl sidled up to Taro and put a coin into the alms can. Taro bowed his head and thanked her. They were about the same height, the little girl and the legless veteran who was my elder brother. Mr Gee dropped to his knee. He raised his camera and began taking pictures.

The sight made my blood boil, just like it had in the hospital when I saw him taking pictures there. Taro had told me that the Americans were studying the radiation damage done by the atom bomb, and the pictures were necessary for science. But this was different. There was no good reason I could see, scientific or otherwise, to take snapshots of my brother's shame. And maybe because we were near the train station, I recalled the candy bar incident, and the arrogant laughter of the American soldiers, and all of us Japanese kids, starving and begging for food and getting only gum and bars of chocolate.

Something inside me snapped. The next thing I knew, I had my arms around Mr Gee's thick American neck. I was clinging to his back like a monkey, trying to pull him to the ground. His camera strap was in my fist, and I was strangling him with it. I wanted to rip the camera from him and crush it in the dirt, as though by destroying his

160

machine I could wipe out all the suffering his photographs contained.

"*Jiro! Yamero!*" Taro yelled. "Stop it now!"

I looked up and saw him coming. I saw my brother push his hands against the ground, trying to get his clumsy wheels in motion. His arms had gotten somewhat stronger since he'd lost his legs. I saw him propel himself awkwardly into the street, not looking either way, not looking out for traffic, as he had so often warned me about. And then I saw the American army truck, careening down the road toward him. My brother was so small on his plank, in the middle of the busy street. His head was even with the truck's enormous fender. There was no way the driver could see him.

But Mr Gee saw him, and the next thing I knew, I was sitting on my backside on the ground, the camera in my hand, and Mr Gee was running full tilt into the traffic toward my brother. He was waving his arms in the air, signalling the truck to stop, but to me, it looked for all the world like he was flying. The truck driver saw them then and screeched on his brakes, but it was too late. The next thing I heard was the sound of splintering wood as Taro's plank was crushed by the truck's massive tyres.

"Taro!" I screamed. I couldn't move. It was as if I had grown roots like a tree. I stared into the street at the big truck. It had stalled now. There was no sign of my brother or Mr Gee. I stood up then. Other cars were stopping too, so I stepped into the street. The truck driver was getting out of the cab. He was wearing an army uniform, and his face was as red and angry as a devil's. I ducked out of his way and tripped over a fist-sized metal object. It was a wheel from Taro's plank. I picked it up. There were scraps of wood on the ground under the truck. I looked for blood. For my brother's body. Instead I heard my brother's laugh.

I ran around the stalled truck toward the sound. It was coming from a deep sewage ditch on the opposite side of the road. When I got to the edge, I looked down.

They were standing waist deep in the murky, stinking water, or they would have been, only Taro couldn't stand. Instead, he had his arm around Mr Gee's shoulders, and the soldier was holding on to him, keeping him above the surface. Taro said something, and now Mr Gee laughed. It was strange to hear my brother speaking English.

"Taro?"

He looked up and saw me and extended his arm.

"Hey, kid. Give me a hand."

I grabbed on to him and pulled as hard as I could. Tarc's arms and torso were stronger than ever, and soon he was safely out.

"I thought the truck had hit you!" I cried.

Mr Gee was standing beside us now. His uniform was sopping wet, and he stank of sewage. Taro spoke to him again and bowed deeply, then he turned to me.

"You must apologize to him."

"What!"

"You must apologize for attacking him. You must thank him for saving my life."

I couldn't believe what I was hearing. The Americans were our enemy. They were the ones who had dropped the bombs that had killed our father. They were the ones who'd blown off my brother's legs.

"No! I'm not apologizing to any stupid American! I wish I'd killed him!"

Taro's eyes flashed, and I thought he was going to hit me, but he didn't. Instead he reached out and grabbed the back of my neck. His fingers were like iron. I said his arms had gotten stronger, but I hadn't realized how strong. He gripped my neck and forced my head to bow, and then my knees to bend. He pushed my forehead down until it touched the ground. He held me there, pressing. Stones bit into my skin.

"Apologize now," he said, "or you are not my brother."

And so I did. "I'm sorry," I mumbled.

"Again. Louder. And say thank you too."

"*I'm sorry!*" I yelled. "*I'm sorry! Thank you! I'm sorry! Thank you!*" The tears were streaming down my face when he finally let me go.

"Good boy," Taro said. "Now give him back his camera."

I wanted to hurl the camera under the wheels of a passing truck. I wanted to throw it into the American's broad, bewildered face. Instead, I held it out. It dangled from the strap. Mr Gee said something. Taro nodded.

"He wants you to take our picture," my brother said.

They stood side by side, or rather, the American squatted down so they'd be the same height. I located the two of them in the camera's viewfinder. My hands were trembling. Mr Gee put his arm around my brother's shoulders, and the two of them grinned. I hated them both.

Then they shook hands and I gave back the camera, and Mr Gee insisted on shaking my hand too. His palm was huge and sweaty, and when no one was looking, I wiped it off on my jacket.

"His name is George," Taro told me. "But you must call him Gee-san."

It sounded like "ji-san", which means "uncle" in Japanese. "He's no uncle of mine," I muttered, but no one was paying any attention.

We searched the area for the remains of Taro's plank. I still had one of the wheels. We found only two others. Taro tried to make light of it, but I knew he was worried. Without the plank on wheels, there was no way for him to get around. I was still too small and could manage only a few blocks with my brother on my back, but then I would get tired and have to put him down to rest. If he couldn't get to his corner to beg for alms, we would have even less to eat.

That night, Gee-san carried him home with ease, stumbling only slightly when the road was pitted. They looked like two college friends who'd gone out drinking and had a bit too much saké. I followed behind, cursing my weakness. They were speaking in English, so I couldn't understand a word they were saying. They sounded like imbeciles, talking gibberish. People stared as they passed us on the street. I was ashamed.

I can't remember how I came to change my mind about Gee-san. Maybe it was when he showed up at our rooming house a few days later with a brand-new plank for Taro. It had four shiny new wheels on the bottom, and a padded cushion on the top, with straps made of leather so Taro could hang on to the sides. It also had a rope for pulling, and a tall pole with a bright red flag on top, so drivers could see us coming through the traffic.

Or maybe it was when he started giving our mother extra rations of food, and for the first time since the war, I had almost enough to eat.

Or maybe it was the night he came by our room to show Taro the photographs he'd taken in Hiroshima and Nagasaki of the atomic bomb victims there. He sat next to Taro at the low desk where my brother studied his books, and they let me sit beside them. The desk lamp shed a circle of light across the stack of black-and-white photographs. There were pictures of young girls and boys my age, pictures of babies and old women and men, but their burns were so bad, they barely looked like human beings any more. It was horrible to see.

Then there were other pictures, not of people, but the shadows of people. Ash-coloured shapes, left on benches, on sidewalks. Like ghosts.

Gee-san was explaining something to my brother. I tugged Taro's sleeve.

"What is it?" I asked.

"The blast from the bomb was so hot, they turned into shadows," Taro said. "That's all that was left of them."

Gee-san's eyes filled with tears.

"I am sorry," he said, in broken Japanese. "This is my country's shame."

Taro nodded. "The shame belongs to all of us."

Our mother's health was failing. She was very unhappy, living in the tiny room in the boarding house in Tokyo, but we didn't have money for a bigger room, or for the train fare back to Sapporo. Day by day, our mother grew sadder, and we worried that she might just fade away completely.

"Oh, I miss Sapporo," she would sigh. "If only I could set eyes upon the Japan Sea once more before I die. . ."

"Be patient," Taro told her. "I'll take you home, you'll see." But when he turned away from her, I saw the hopelessness in his eyes.

Then one afternoon Gee-san came to meet us at our street corner just as we were getting ready to leave. He seemed very excited, and his cheeks were pink. He started talking fast. Taro listened for a while, then he shook his head. Gee-san started talking again, even faster, but Taro turned his back.

"Jiro," he said to me sharply. "Let's go."

"Wait," I said. I looked up at Gee-san. He was standing there, watching us, looking large and helpless. "What did he say?"

"Nothing. He said he found me a job. I told him I already had a job." Taro held up his alms can and shook it. A few coins rattled inside.

Gee-san shrugged and stuck his hands in his pockets and turned to go.

"What kind of job?" I persisted, watching him walk away.

"Helping the Americans," Taro said. "In a laboratory. I told him I couldn't possibly help –"

But I didn't hear the rest. "*Matte!*" I shouted to Gee-san. "Wait!"

And that was that. It turned out that Gee-san had talked to the army doctors who were studying the effects of atomic radiation on people, and they knew some scientists who were studying the effects of atomic radiation on plants. They needed a translator and a laboratory assistant to help out with the experiments. Taro knew the words for all the plants in Japanese and English and Latin, and he was familiar with the lab procedures too. Of course at first he didn't want to do it, but I convinced him. It was necessary for science, I explained, and eventually he agreed. Gee-san persuaded them to let me tag along and be his legs. We were a team, Taro and me, and before long, we were able to move our mother into a better apartment.

I even started learning a little English myself.

But still our mother was unhappy, and soon we knew that her end was near.

"It's time," Taro announced. "We have enough money. We're taking her home."

"What about our job?" I asked. "What's Gee-san going to say?"

"Gee-san's coming with us," Taro said, grinning. "He's got some leave and he's taking it with us."

And so it was settled. We must have been a strange sight as we boarded the train, an old bent woman leaning on a skinny boy, a legless Japanese veteran on the back of a towering American GI.

We bought lunch boxes on the train and mandarin oranges, and watched the country pass by our window. Many of the cities we travelled through were in ruins, reduced to rubble by the carpet bombs and the fire bombs. We all fell silent, thinking of the people who had suffered and died. But there were signs of reconstruction too, and houses being built, and the countryside was beautiful, and the young rice was growing in the fields.

We caught a ferry that would take us over the Sea of Japan to the port of Otaru, just west of Sapporo. Our mother was so excited, we could hardly tear her from the railing of the boat as she gazed across the ocean's gentle swell. From Otaru, we travelled to our cousin's house, which overlooked the sea. All the children from the village had heard that we were coming, and they came out to greet us. They surrounded Gee-san and pointed at him and laughed, touching his clothes and crying out "*Gaijin! Gaijin!* A Foreigner! Look!" until finally I had to scold them for their rudeness.

They didn't dare laugh at Taro or even stare at him. Some-how they knew I'd pound them like a rice cake if they did.

It was good to be back, good to be able to walk out of the house and hear the crickets in the bamboo, and clamber down the rocky shoreline to the beach. Gee-san and I carried Taro across the rocks, and we left him on the warm sand with a book, enjoying the sea breeze, while we took a walk along the water's edge. I knew Gee-san only had a very short time for holiday and that he would be leaving us soon. This made me sad. He sensed my sadness, I think, and he put his big hand on top of my head and ruffled my hair.

I twisted out from under his palm. I didn't like to be touched on the head. It made me feel small. He grinned and made a sad face, pulling the corners of his mouth way down, which made me laugh. I still didn't speak very much English, so mostly we communicated like this when Taro wasn't there to translate. Now, he reached into his shirt pocket, pulled out a photograph, and handed it to me.

It was the picture I'd taken of him and my brother after they had climbed out of the sewage ditch. It was a little blurry, but you could see Gee-san squatting next to Taro, and Taro with his arm draped around Gee-san's shoulder, and they were both wet and grinning, like they'd just done something very funny and a little bit naughty, and got away with it. Gee-san pointed to the picture and then to his face.

"Handsome guy," he said.

I didn't think he was handsome at all. I thought he looked

like a pale, hairy ghost, and so I shook my head.

"No, no," I said. "Not handsome guy."

"No?" he said, pretending to be surprised.

"No," I said. "Gee-san not handsome guy. Gee-san is kind-ness man. Gee-san is most kindness man all over world."

He took a step back and blinked his eyes, and I felt tears in my eyes too, so I turned away from him and looked out to sea. Soon he'd be crossing the sea, going home to America, to his own country and family, and leaving me here with mine. I wanted to give him something to remember us by, but I had nothing. I looked down at my feet. There was a little shell in the sand, so I picked it up. It was a pretty golden colour, with a whirly shape and a point at the tip. Taro would know the name, but I didn't. Still, it was all I had, and so I gave it to him.

"Is for you," I said. "So you remember, OK?"

Gee-san laughed. "OK, buddy," he said, tossing the shell in the air. "Thanks."

But I was still sad, and he knew it.

"Hey," he said, holding up the shell. "Tell you what. I'll come back to Sapporo. I'll bring this back to you one of these days."

"It is promise?" I said, squinting up at him.

"Yeah," he said, pocketing the shell. "I promise."

He never did, but that's OK. Maybe he still needs it, to remember.

Chapter 9
AFELA

We went up and down the aisles of Ikku-Mart, doing a big shop for the beach house.

"Grab me some of those beans," said Mum. "Make it four tins – no, those *big* ones below. How many people do you think we're feeding?"

"Oh, of course: six hundred million *billion*." I clanked the tins into the shopping trolley. "The whole flipping world."

"It feels like it, you're right."

"Why couldn't we get the other house, where everyone *fitted*?"

"Someone else got it before us. And pearl barley, Afela. There. Up. To the right. No, the *big* packet. Next year I will book earlier."

"Make sure you do."

"Yes, *boss*! Someone's a crabby pants."

"I hate sharing with Lorelei. She's gone all boy-mad. And I hate Uncle Dorro being in the lounge room all the time and hogging the big screen. And I hate that pig-dog of Sam's too.

It's too big and too loud, just like Sam, and I thought the rule was *no pets*. And—"

Mum rubbed my head. "You're thirteen. It's your job to hate everything. And Uncle Dorro's had a bad year with the divorce and everything, and the business failing; show some kindness."

"He *deserves* a bad year. He deserves a whole bad *life*."

Mum looked along the shelves for something.

"With spiky knobs on it," I added.

She woke up to me, smiled, and smacked a kiss on to my forehead. She tore off the bottom half of her shopping list and gave it to me. "Here, sweet. You pick out the fruit and veg and we'll be done in half the time."

"Aww? Do I *haff* to?"

"Did I give you a choice?" She fluttered her eyelashes at me.

I made a big show of glumly mooching off. But actually, when I got to the fruit and veg section, it was nice, all dim and cool. Everything looked really fresh, the cucumbers shiny green, the tomatoes plump and dewy. The peaches and nectarines practically glowed in their heaps, smelling wonderful. I chose and bagged some, sniffing each one before I put it in the bag.

I was totally absorbed in what I was doing until someone reached for the same peach as I did, and our hands – mine melting-pot light brown, hers paler – knocked together.

"Sorry," we both said.

"Oh, Emily!" I tried to change my tone of voice in

172

the middle so that I didn't sound so dismayed.

"Oh, hi, Afela!" She didn't smile. Emily Danziger doesn't *do* smiling. "I didn't know you were down here for the holidays."

"I didn't know *you* were!" Which wasn't exactly true. More like, I'd forgotten to keep a lookout and avoid her. "Where are you staying?" As I asked, I saw the place, the pale spacious rooms, the bush and the sea framed in the picture windows.

"High Huskisson. It's away from the beach, but it's got a good outlook. What about you?"

"We're at High Vincentia, like every year. Same old crowd of rellies all shouting their heads off." I rolled my eyes.

Emily nodded politely. It always unnerved me, that she didn't *just know*, the way I *just knew* about her. Was she pretending? Was she laughing at me? I never knew. I always felt embarrassed with her, as if I laughed and chatted too much while she stayed serious and watchful.

I chose a couple more peaches so it wouldn't look as if I were running away from her, and then I said, "Well, better get this lot back to Mum. See you round!"

"Bye." Did she sound relieved too? Or puzzled? Did she think I was rude?

The rest of the supermarket circuit, I kept an eye out for her. I thought, *We'll get stuck behind her and her dad at the checkout, I just know, and Mum will be all like, "Hello, Marcus! Emily, how lovely! Santa bring you lots of presents?" And Emily will be too well-mannered to boast about the two-metre Seeg screen she got for her bedroom, or the whole new horse-*

riding outfit from the London tailor, with the handmade boots. So it'll end up the grown-ups talking and Em and me standing about trying not to meet each other's eyes. Awful.

But maybe Emily was keeping a lookout too. When I saw her next she was way off at the furthest register, and then she and her dad (and her mum too – for some reason even that made me burn, the whole family being there, so complete and self-contained) sailed out of the supermarket while we were still waiting our turn in the queue.

Finally we wheeled our trolley into the car park. The sky was still grey and the air was almost *cold* – it was supposed to be summer! – and there was an irritating breeze. The Buggy was full of my squabbling brothers and cousins, I could see from metres away. Sam had let his horrible dog Mack out of the back, and Mack was going around weeing on everything, the poor half-dead plants in the car park dividers, the Buggy's wheels, sniff-sniff, wee-wee. And Sam was ignoring him, talking to someone in a car, a silver-haired woman – was it Grandma Grace? I knew we were expecting her.

She drove off before we got there and it was all fetch-that-dog and where's-Nyente and quieten-down-in-the-back-there for-a-while. We crammed the shopping into the Buggy, on people's laps and around their legs because we couldn't put it in the back with Mack. Then Nyente and Aunty Sloe came back from the chemist's and somehow fitted themselves in among us, and off we drove through the sprawling suburbs of Nowra.

The sky was grey – it was almost cold outside! – and everything looked shabby and depressing.

"Was that lady related to us?" I said to Sam, because I didn't like sitting next to him and I thought he must be sensing it.

"What lady?"

"The one you were talking to, in the car."

"Related? Why the heck would she be related to us?"

"I don't know. She *looked* related. She frowned just like Grandma Grace does."

"Bull, she did. She wasn't even the same *colour*!" Sam said to me.

"Not the same as you or me, maybe. But Grandma Grace is as pale as that, easily."

"No, Afela," Mum said loudly. "The lady was a stranger to Sam. End of fight."

"I'm not fighting. Sam's just being an idiot."

"*You're* being a—"

"What did she want, Sam? The woman?" said Mum, meaning, *Why on earth did you start this, Afela?*

"She wanted to know how to get to Vincentia."

"*High* Vincentia?"

"I guess," said Sam. "She was American; maybe she didn't know about the high towns."

I snorted. "Like the sea didn't rise in America too?"

"She may just not be a coastal person," Mum said tiredly.

"Anyway," Sam went on, "I said, 'What you want to go there

for? It's a dump.'" Even he realized how rude that sounded, so he rushed on. "'Plenty prettier places for a tourist to visit. Plenty better waves.' But she's got some business there, she reckons."

"Now she's seen *you*, she has," said my cousin Arthur suggestively. He used to be cute, but now that he's twelve he's just smutty-minded.

"Yes, now she's seen Sexy Sam." Nyente grinned at Sam from the front seat.

And it got sillier from there.

So we drove back to Weston, the boringest and ugliest and smallest beach house in High Vincentia and possibly the world, which has no "outlook" like Emily's place, but which is near the beach, at least – although the beach isn't fabulous, having never been tidied up for tourists after the flooding that ate the edges off all the beach towns in the 2030s. Grandma Grace had arrived while we were out, and Sam was right, she looked nothing like that lady in the car, and everyone was talking over the top of each other in the kitchen with excitement. I went and threw myself on my bed and groaned with boredom, until Lorelei told me to shut up because she was text-text-texting, Miss Busy Fingers, to all her best friends back home, and she couldn't text and listen at the same time because in the last year her brain has all drained out of her head and into her bra, hasn't it? And because it was so grey and not-summery, all the littlies had decided it would be more fun to crash around in the house and yell, or scream

176

around in the yard, than it would to go down to the beach and let us have a bit of peace around here. And Uncle Dorro's quiz show was bellowing out so that he could hear it above the cousins, and – well, everything was pretty much unbearable. I stared out the window at the clouds, which were like crowds of grey bottom cheeks hanging over the town. I stared at the ruffled jingle shells I'd collected my first day here and piled on the windowsill. When I'd seen them on the sand I couldn't not pick them up, they were so bright and pearly – some white, some clear, some pale, pale orange; they were like money lying there. They didn't look nearly so good now, not nearly as irresistible. They were like dried-out bones, or loosened fingernails. Either side of them I'd lined up the worst bunch of holiday presents I've ever been given – a T-shirt from Aunty Sloe that I wouldn't be seen dead in, a music chip from my sister Kola that I already had, that kind of thing. Finally I picked up the worst present, the camera. I opened its box as slowly as if I was defusing a bomb, and slid out its little manual and opened it with a sigh.

Me and cameras, we've never got on. Mum knows this – or at least, I thought she knew. I hate cameras the way some people hate balloons – if there's one in the room, I can't relax; I'm too scared it'll go off *pop*. There are no good pictures of me in the world; in all of them I look like some kind of cornered animal, all hunched up and bug-eyed, desperate to run away.

"I figured you just need to get on the other side of one for a while." Mum had beamed when I took the box out of the wrapping paper and stared at it, thinking, *It can't be.* "It's a great way to express yourself. And useful for school projects," she finished lamely, watching my face and seeing the struggle there.

It's all right, I was polite. I had a rough idea how much the camera cost. I would never *say* how lame this year's presents were. And it wasn't as if I *wanted* riding boots or a Seeg screen. I didn't know what I wanted. Just . . . not this. Just not –

Histogram showing the distribution of tones in the image. Horizontal axis corresponds to pixel brightness – I scowled into the manual, willing it to make sense.

Crash! went something in the boys' room, behind Lorelei. "Oh, for heaven's *sake!*" She flung down her phone, stomped in there, and started screeching at them.

OK, that was *my* last straw. I snatched up the camera in its pouch and got out of there. It was like fighting my way out from the eye of a cyclone: Lorelei screeched; the kitchen full of rellies chattered and shouted with laughter; Uncle Dorro's game show yabbered; the cousins yelled commando commands in the bushes out the front. Sam was out there too, playing *my*-stick with Mack, hanging tight on to the stick as Mack bounced and growled on the other end. What was wrong with people that they had to have so much noise around? What was wrong with a bit of peace and quiet? My hand shook with anger as it closed the gate behind me. *What's wrong with you,* said a little voice in my head, *that the noise is bothering you so badly?*

I walked up the hill out of town, toward the roundabout. I wouldn't meet anyone there. I breathed deeply and was Emily for a few moments; she was cutting pictures out of magazines, shapes out of coloured paper, there at the big table in her near empty beach house. The view sat peaceful and airy in the picture windows. Every now and again her parents murmured to each other, or turned a page of their newspapers with a rustle –

No, even that noise was like sandpaper on my skin. What I'd like, I thought as I stalked uphill past the site where GREEN-SCENE ECO-RESPONSIBLE HOMES was putting up new houses, would be to keep walking, right out of High Vincentia and on up the road into the bush, on up into the mountains. Walk away from all people – not just my family, but *all* the irritating, messy people of the world. Leave them all behind. Stop, and stay where I stopped, and live there by myself, in a cave or in a house made of branches, and walk out at night under the stars to a high place, where I'd look down across the shadowy hills – nothing but animals there, whispering along in the leaf mould, nothing but birds refolding their wings in their sleep – and see the houses and the little towns, twinkling to themselves in the night, and know that I never had to go back.

The roundabout was a mound of grey concrete, a gleaming reflector-line all around it. It looked like a spaceship, parked there in its circle of new black asphalt in the middle of the grey and orange earth that the road-upgrading machinery had broken up, edged with trashed bush and piled-up scrub refuse.

I got out the camera and turned it on – *beep*. The spaceship hovered on the screen. Ugly, ugly, ugly – how ugly people made the world, leaving these big scars in the bushland! How I wished –

I pressed the button to take the picture.

And I changed the universe.

It took a few seconds. Everything was soft for a moment, and I cut through existence like a bright, sharp knife slicing a sponge cake. Then some things firmed back to normal, while others stayed soft, and it was like looking through a smudged window for a moment. Then the smudges cleared; all the adjustments were made, and she was standing in the middle of the concrete roundabout, with her back to me and her long, crinkly red hair spread out like a flag on the breeze. I had imagined dark and streaky clothes on to her, with threads and webs blowing off them. She had bare white legs, strong white feet. I couldn't see her face, but I knew it was pale and freckly, with blind-looking pale blue eyes. She came from the Scottish bit of me, not the Malian or the Polish or the Irish-by-way-of-American parts that had all been mixed into my family history since the first Scottish ancestors came out here to Australia way, way back.

I had peeled her off myself, dragged her up out of my melting-pot gene pool, and I had set her outside myself. She shared my birth date, and she had a past that led from that date to this one. I could walk up and down her past in my mind and examine it like an art gallery full of VD-O installations. She would go on just as long as I did, and die at the moment I died.

The red-haired girl walked away, off the roundabout and along the road inland. The soles of her feet were black with dirt, even though these were the first steps she'd ever taken.

I sat on the kerb and shook and swore to myself. The universe pressed in close around me, full of swarms and hollows. I could look at any part of it and see how it was put together.

I did this before, remember? I wanted to be an only child, so I made Emily Danziger. It was someone's birthday, and Dad forced me to be in a family photo – you can see in that photo how angry I was – and the moment it was taken I split, just like this. I peeled lucky Emily off myself, and there she was, in the photo and in life – I remember that cake-cutting feeling, the scary softness of all things – then, all of a sudden Emily was there, and her mum and dad were there too, and tiny changes had been made to the past, like a line of dominoes knocking one another down, so that Emily and her parents could exist.

And now I'd done it again, and the red-haired girl was disappearing down the far side of the hill, on her way to her wild life in the bush. And just as I lived an only child's life through Emily, I would live this wild one with the red-haired girl, seeing the stars and the creatures through her eyes, feeling heat and cold and rain and breezes through her skin.

My scalp still creeping, I stared at the displayed image, the girl on the spaceship, her hair and her clothes floating. Then I beeped the camera off, and put it in its pouch, and hung it around my neck. I got up and walked away, down through the town and along the seawall. The sandy beach and the two lines of half-buried house wrecks; I hardly saw them for watching my mind try to make sense of what I'd done, what I'd found out – found out *again* – that I could do. Was it magic? Could magic really happen, then?

Far along the wall I saw familiar figures: Sam, walking Mack. I felt relieved; I almost didn't hate them any more. I would go and swap insults with Sam and everything would start to feel more normal. I walked faster to catch up with them.

The two of them reached the top of the stairs down to the beach, and Mack ran down and set off across the sand fast, straight for the water. Oops, no, he was running *at someone*, someone who'd just come into sight behind that dead holiday house up to its windowsills in sand. She was walking along the water's edge gazing out to sea. She didn't see Mack hurtling toward her.

"Mack, no!" I called out. He didn't have a hope of hearing me.

He crashed past the woman's ankles, knocking her over. He skittered back and clamped his jaws on her leg and dragged her, shaking her leg the way he shakes the stick in the *my*-stick game with Sam.

The woman's shout reached me, tiny with the distance. I started to run. Sam was already halfway down the beach, shouting and waving his arms. By the time I reached them, he had stopped right by Mack, but he wasn't doing anything to make Mack let go.

"I'm so sorry, I'm so sorry!" he peeped over and over, like a stuck voice-simulator, and he spread his hands helplessly to either side at the sight of foaming, toothy Mack, who kept on shaking the woman's leg, gurgly growling, mad.

"Please call your dog off." The woman spoke so firmly and reasonably, it would have been funny if Mack hadn't been so monstrous in the middle of us, if there hadn't been actual blood showing through the holes his teeth had ripped in the woman's blue jeans leg.

I grabbed Mack's collar. I smacked his nose as hard as I could. In the deepest, growliest voice I could find in myself I said, "Mack! Drop it!" and I hit his nose again.

And he did. He dropped the leg.

I threw my weight back to drag him far enough away that he wouldn't pick it up again. The woman was scrambling away, but she couldn't walk properly; a little wave hit her leg and the foam splashed up red.

"Give me your T-shirt, Sam," I said, "to sop up the blood."

I held Mack's collar as his slimy, bloodied head jerked back and forth, while Sam ("Oh, God, oh, God!") wrestled off his jacket and shirt. "Here." Out of the corner of my eye I saw the shirt flapping.

"Take this dog," I said, snatching the shirt. "He's too strong for me. Take him right away!"

And then Sam was hauling Mack up the sand, and my arms, which had just about been ripped out of their sockets, were wrapping the T-shirt around the woman's leg, covering up the torn flesh, covering up a glimpse of bone.

"He shouldn't have a dog like that, if he can't control it," the woman said, lying back and speaking shakily to the sky.

"He thinks it's some kind of fashion accessory, like that jacket or the sunglasses," I said. "He's got no idea – well, I guess he's got an idea *now* – what a dog like that can do."

"You know him?"

"He's my cousin." I knotted the shirt in place and looked up at her.

She was the lady from the car park, the American Sam had been talking to. Her silver hair was clumped with wet sand, and her face was even paler now than the first time I'd seen her. She propped herself up on her elbows to look at the blood-smeared T-shirt.

"I think you should just lie there for a bit," I said. "Get over the shock. Here, put your head in my lap." I crawled up and brushed some of the sand out of her hair.

"They're coming!" came Sam's stressed-out voice. He was high up on the soft sand, waving his mobile. "Ambulance is coming!" Mack was tied to a railing on the seawall, resting as if after a job well done.

I gave Sam a thumbs-up and settled the woman's head on my lap.

"I'll have to cancel Antarctica," she said.

"I'm sorry?"

"I was on my way to Antarctica. I'll have to cancel."

Antarctica, along this beach? It took me a moment to make sense of her. "You never know," I said, pushing that glimpse of bone out of my head – it hadn't been *broken* bone, after all – "they might be able to stitch you up and let you out of hospital straight away." I looked into her upside-down face. "Hi, I'm Afela," I said.

She smiled. "Hello, Afela. Thank you very much for the use of your lap. My name's Margaret. I'm from the US, you've probably guessed."

"I saw you this morning, talking to Sam in the car park at Nowra. He said you've got some business to do, here in High Vincentia?"

"Oh, yes." She touched her jeans pocket, and looked out to sea. "I was so close to finishing. Argentina, Australia – and Antarctica's the last. But it figures that this would happen here, of all places. This town is a disaster zone for Henschlers."

Henschlers? I almost said. The name snagged on memories so vague I had to sit awhile and chase them down: an afternoon so boring and rainy that the local history museum had looked like an exciting option – better than hanging around at the beach house, anyway; a printed-out news story, slipping down in its frame on the wall, the blurred face of the guy who'd not died, but just disappeared in the air accident off the coast, in some spooky way, so that there wasn't any wreckage for the experts to work out what happened. Henschler, John or Jacob or some name starting with J. I remember thinking he had a really old-fashioned, all-American face, good straight teeth, smiling and frowning into the sunshine.

"It must be great to go travelling overseas," I said, to get that sad look off her face. "So long as you're not attacked by savage dogs, I mean."

"You haven't been outside Australia, Afela?"

"No, but one day I will. Or –" The camera, the sponge-cake feeling, the red-haired girl slipped back into my mind. "– If I want it badly enough, maybe I could even. . ."

Her voice broke in on my thoughts. "You could what, honey?"

I looked down at her. I couldn't tell this kind, sensible-looking lady that I was magic, could I? That I was actually three people so far? That I might become any number more before I died?

Then again, we might never meet again. And she might just think she'd been delirious and misheard me. And there was no one else I could tell.

"Do you think it's possible," I said carefully, "for one person to . . . to live a whole lot of different lives in the one life?" There, that wasn't quite telling it, wasn't quite *not* telling.

She lay perfectly still, looking up at me. Then she reached into the pocket of her jeans. "Here. I want you to do something for me." She put a shell into my hand. "Go down and throw this in the sea, as far out as you can."

I looked from the shell to her clear eyes and back. The shell was pale orange, just like the ones on my windowsill, all dried out and dull. There were at least seven other shells like it in the sand around her, all wetter and brighter than this one. "A jingle shell?"

"Throw it in the sea for me."

"In the sea? Now?"

She half sat up again. "Go down, while I watch, and throw it as hard as you can. Then come back here, and I'll see if I can explain."

It's the middle of the night. I'm in the front seat of the Buggy. The country slips by outside, scraggly black trees, moonlit branches, starry sky. It's restful after all those hours in the hospital under the fluoro lights. Dad's put his music on; we finished talking a few kilometres back. Now I can relax and let my head fill with all the things I couldn't tell him, that Margaret told me.

George Keane, his name was. Any Internet search will bring him up: George Keane, photojournalist. I'm not sure I want to look. After all, I'm descended from the part of George Keane that didn't *want* to be George Keane, the part that hated cameras and what they could show, the part that wanted to settle down here at the end of the world where there were no wars and no famines, and change his name, and be the man Dad's been telling me about, with a big multicultural family that he could hide in the middle of, and a job with the council, and trips to the football or the boxing as regular as an atomic clock.

No one will understand, who hasn't seen it for themselves, Margaret said to me. *I've found it's best to keep quiet about all of this. People don't like to think they're descended from a figment of someone's imagination.*

No, she's right, we don't. Even having seen such things happen twice now, I don't like to think that Margaret's grandfather created my great-great-grandfather, when he came to Australia all ill and depressed after taking those pictures of the world's troubles. People are supposed to grow from almost nothing, from a single zygote dividing into two, and dividing again into four, and so on. That's the normal way it goes; you don't get to be thirteen without seeing it happen on those "Reproduction and Relationship" VD-Os a few times.

But it's not as if Great-Great-Grandpa was any less of a person for being created a different way from normal. Is a starfish not a proper starfish because it's grown from the broken-off leg of another starfish? And think about those clones from the 2020s; didn't they all end up getting full citizenship and human rights and stuff? Emily and the red-haired girl are their own people, even if I can watch their lives and feel all the sensations they feel, alongside my own, like different channels on a television.

Is that magic, that I can do that? I'd whispered to Margaret, in Casualty.

I don't know what it is, she murmured back. *That "peeling off" that you talk about, it's as real a process as cell division, isn't it? You and I know that; Grandpa Gee knew it. It's just that science isn't big enough to explain it yet, and without a scientific explanation a lot of things look like magic. Or madness, Afela. Be careful who you tell about this, if anyone. People can be very cruel.*

I'll be careful. I close my eyes on the rushing darkness. I've spent so long looking at Margaret's face today, that she's right there behind my eyelids, talking or dozing or listening in her polite way. She's almost as real as Emily Danziger's comfortable bed and spacious bedroom in the dark holiday house at High Huskisson, almost as real as the warm nest of leaves in the cave where the red-haired girl sleeps, almost as real as this not-quite-comfortable-enough seat, with the safety belt digging into my cheek, as I settle against the headrest, almost as real as my dad singing tunelessly along to his terrible country music, as he follows the highway home.

Chapter 10
MARGARET

Margaret Keane Henschler hadn't slept well in a decade. She didn't expect to any longer either. So she wasn't bothered by the muffled sounds of the hotel corridor: guests departing for punishingly early flights, or late-night revellers whispering, fumbling, giggling as they staggered back from one of the corporate venues (the Olde Pub, the Olde Oyster Bar, the Olde Discotheque, etc.).

Her room was northerly, as she liked it, and high up – even the express vertical monorail took twenty minutes from standstill liftoff at ground level to reach this magnificent height. Stage 215.

As she puttered about in the complimentary air-chair, making herself a cup of yellow tea and checking the postings on her dedicated Ikon, she glanced from time to time out the broad oval window. Several layers of cloud blanket hovered between her and the ground, but the blankets were loose knit ones, always unravelling, and the lights of brave Nutu showed far below. Not as pinpricks, the way she remembered cities of her youth, from the vantage points of airplanes or skyscraper observation decks, but as a warm, constant, seeping blur. A kind of phosphorescence, as of some beast hovering near the bottom of the sea, biding its time with patience and mystery and an implicit clarity of intention.

It was her first visit to Nutu, and – she logged on to her blood profile to see how those letheocyte cells were faring, not great – it was likely to be her last. She ought to get some sleep. It would be a busy day. A district manager had promised to send her a guide on the early side, and before the formal opening at 19:30 Margaret would be treated to an hour's tour of the urban nexus. Then she'd have to square her shoulders and look as lively as an old bird could do when she was pre-sented to whichever Minor Panjandrum had been assigned to open the show.

And *that* event would be taxing as well as tiring. She would have to keep her opinions to herself and let the images do the talking.

"Not good at that, much, am I," she muttered, wishing for a minute she had chosen gin instead of tea.

"Indistinct for purposes of legal record," replied the Ikon. "Please repeat with increased volume and emphasis."

She disconnected the Logometer, which was quite possibly illegal, but at her age she could feign all kinds of incapacities and dotty logic and get away with murder.

Her bloodwork was disheartening. Those painful transfu-sions, two in the last year alone, and the implanting of a portal in her navel for the convenient delivery of medication. When

191

she washed, sitting on a plastic stool in the shower stall, she rinsed the aperture with her eyes closed, pretending she was a girl again playing doctor. The decontaminant, a local radiation she could apply herself with a silver-nozzled hose, smelled of shallots sizzled too long in the pan until they were dried and caramelized. Or maybe that was her own native smell after all these years. She was caramelized herself, by infirmity and age and sheer stubborn animal endurance.

"Meggsie?" The panel to the adjoining chamber slid open. "I thought I heard you up. You all right?"

"I was being quiet as a mouse. I hope I didn't disturb you, dear."

"May I come in?"

Margaret beckoned with a smile she feared was less than fully warm. She loved her great-niece, but she also loved the privacy of midnight. "Of course, Iona. I can make this teabag stretch to a second cup, a weak one, if you'd like. Was I talking to myself again?"

"Your little twitter? I'd sleep through *that*. No, it was traffic in the hall outside. Must've been some wedding; there's silver confetti in the hall and someone dropped a trodden bouquet. I looked."

Margaret heated a second cone of water, and the teabag swam again. "You're dreadfully sweet to come with me all this way. I do wish you'd taken yourself downstairs to avail yourself of whatever passes for entertainment these days. I feel I've chained you up here. I'm really quite competent, you know.

Everything's at my fingertips on the Ikon, and I live on very little sleep. It's a skill the aged have. I think it's called 'biding one's time'."

"I have far too much opportunity to party. I'd rather bide your time with you."

"Sweetly said." And genuinely meant, to be sure: Margaret knew that Iona was a devoted girl and a kind one. "But if you tend to me night and day, I feel I ought to be uttering words of wisdom – making it worth your while. Either that, or leaving you a packet of money. And the fiscal codes prohibit that, as you know."

"Don't talk about leaving me anything. Don't talk about leaving, period."

Fair enough. Margaret herself had always felt the same.

She allowed Iona to finish the brewing of tea. It was a gift the elderly could give, to let the young feel competent as they lunged and fussed and mismanaged things. The steam rising from the tisane made Iona's pretty face florid and ripe, her stray-away hair curl further. "I do hope you will go to a wedding one day," said Margaret. "Your own, I mean."

"Now, Meggsie—"

"I'm old, I can say things like that. Don't take offence."

"*You* never married. And what a life you've had!"

"And what a life I have had, indeed. And what a life I haven't."

She didn't regret it, the turning down of marriage proposals – of dear John, dear John! – who in any case had died the following year – or of that improbable rascal, Mr Shamas Nirouz, when she'd lived in Mombasa in her twenties. Nor did she forget the lovers, whose names she had never committed to the airwaves, for their safety and for her pride. But that business of leaving a child –

"Yes, leaving a child means, in the end, leaving a child, I suppose," said Iona. "I take your point."

"I was talking my thoughts aloud again. Shame on me," said Margaret. "I can't always tell. I hope I never say anything unflattering or unkind. You are very dear to me, Iona; you do know that."

Iona didn't need to answer. She cradled the beverage in her hands and said, "Are you looking forward to sightseeing?"

"Are my eyes going, or did they build Nutu intentionally blurry?"

Iona laughed. "Atmospheric perspective. I bet even the pyramids looked fuzzy to the occasional crocodile passing by and looking up."

"Or whatever ancient Eyptian ibis goddess happened to look down. I think," continued Margaret, "at least I *thought* I could see the gel simulacrum of the Manhattan skyline just before I retired last night. At least, what I saw resembled it enough that I could apply my memories of old New York to it. It served. I imagined I heard a little jazz in the stratosphere, and smelled burning pretzels and chestnuts, and the stink of diesel. Funny how smells last the longest."

"Does it make you sad?"

"One thing standing in for another? No. Homage is a legitimate exercise. After all, New York was New Amsterdam once, standing in for old Amsterdam; and New England had to make do for the old retired country left behind by pilgrims and plunderers. Nutu can be fully itself and still hearken back to New York, all at the same time." She laughed. "At least it can to me. Lucky me: I *knew* the old New York, back then. Before the Events."

"I want to go to the Statue of Liberty. I've heard they installed a new harbour around her, and they got the salt spray just right. And seagulls."

"Hmmm. Perhaps I'll skip that one. Lip service to Liberty isn't my cup of tea. . ."

Iona pulled a frown and raised her eyebrows. "I turned off the Logometer, dear," said Margaret. "Not to worry."

"You don't know if there are internal Logometers," said Iona, indicating the panelled ceiling.

"No I don't," said Margaret, "but if there are, cheers, everyone." She raised her tea in a kind of toast. "Here's to Nutu: NewYorkTwo: the pride of the plains. 'Start spreading the news; I'm leaving today. . .'"

But she was alarming her dear, law-abiding niece – no, great-niece – and so she stopped. "I never could carry a tune," she admitted. "Come, darling, I think you should go try to sleep again. Tomorrow will be a long day and a fine one, and you may never come back here again. I want you to remember what you see, not be bleary and yawning because you stayed awake to keep me company. Pack it in now; off with you. Do you want a sleeping nostrum?"

"I don't need drugs. I read Dickens. . ."

"Dickens to doze by? The young are different from us: insane! Now leave me be. I insist."

Iona drained her cone and set it aside. "All right. But tap at the door if you feel a sudden yen for company. It happens, you know. And that's why I'm here. One day I will want to remember that I could help you when you asked. . ."

"Nonsense, don't romanticize me or yourself either," said Margaret briskly. "Don't tell stories, darling; tell the truth. You're here, a dutiful lovely thing, but I'll be cross with us both if that prevents you from getting your sleep. Now off with you."

Still, she kissed Iona with uncommon gentleness, delaying the brush of her lips against the girl's blossomy cheek.

Iona hesitated as the door slid halfway closed, then stopped with electronically programmed courtesy as it sensed the reticence in the departing guest. "Meggsie?"

"I've never liked that name, 'Meggsie'," said Margaret, "and that was a thought I intended you to hear, by the way. But I let you use it because it is your private code for me. Your grandfather loved you very much, you know, Iona. My brother Jason could be quite a piece of work, believe me – I still argue with him in my dreams – but he loved his granddaughter to distraction, and so do I now that he's gone."

Iona was just looking at her, somewhat moonily.

"I used to be called Maggie. I liked that," said Margaret,

relenting. "But I interrupted you, Iona. What did you want?"

"Oh, nothing," said Iona. "I suppose – well, good night."

"Good morning, in a minute, if you don't get to bed."

Margaret was relieved to be alone again. Oh, the eagerness of the young! And a good thing too, she lectured herself, but they did wear on one so.

She should sleep too, she knew it, but every sleep could easily be the last one. The doctors were quite clear on that. And while she wasn't at all scared of death – at least not yet; she might change her mind about that in the final moments – she still wanted to savour what she could.

A light rain was falling below, she guessed. She could see lightning flashing through the clouds. As a girl, she'd never imagined she'd see lightning from above, like a jagged fishing line scraping down the walls of air to stab at the ground, or a tree, or a poor human in the wrong place at the lightning time.

The things we see in our handful of days!

But seeing was everything, wasn't it? That was why she was here.

She propelled her air-chair back to the service wall and pressed a few instructions on the pad. She was happy to dissolve the shimmery image of stars reflected in water – fairly corny for such an upscale establishment as this – as the wall uploaded from her Ikon the array of reproductions she'd chosen. Chosen, supervised, arranged, negotiated, contracted, and was here at last to celebrate tomorrow – well, today – at the Nutu NuMuseum of Modern Art.

Photography had died fifty years ago, and from her position as a retired ambassador, Margaret had argued for a comeback. Her advanced age and her former station – though there were no ambassadors any longer, not in the new order – had served in her interest. She'd pulled strings. She'd made it happen.

And so this was something of a vanity show. She knew that full well. But she hoped nonetheless that it might have validity for the young artist, for the student moving through galleries trying to pick up a lover. Photography used to be reliable, or at least more reliable than it now was. It used to tell us something that, from at least one single point, revealed one glimpse, one of the many aspects of truth.

A hidden aspect, a secret aspect, perhaps. Fair enough. But truth nonetheless, even if unknowable. An outmoded concept today, both culturally and technologically. Today, if all images could be changed at will, no images could stare back at one, full of mystery and integrity. Integrity *because* of mystery – exactly so.

The title of the show flashed up: *The Keane Gene: We Are a Camera Too.*

She'd insisted on "Too" instead of "Tu". What an antediluvian she'd become!

George "Gee" Keane.

Jason Keane Henschler.
Iona Keane Henschler.

Dear Iona, so proud to be part of this! And she had what it took, if Margaret could trust herself. And after a lifetime spent potting about with academics and museum management and cultural diplomacy, Margaret trusted herself rather fully. Iona's eye needed maturing, of course, but whose didn't? All in good time.

It's all in knowing what to leave out, she began to lecture an invisible crowd; but then she felt a pang, suddenly, and an uncharacteristic flush of emotion: *Oh, but one can't afford to leave anything out!*

That word *leave* again. Iona had tripped her up with cloying sentimentality.

Let the images speak for themselves, she said, finishing the lecture with a thump of the imaginary podium. She directed the images to bleed up and recede on to the matte-finish wall.

CLICK.

Tiger Woods. Not the autographed one, the standard-issue photo op, but a quick study, a snap. "Tiger Woods". A man who looked like an ambulatory sapling, with limbs so limber he might splay in half and never stop smiling. Gee had caught him balancing a sports rod of some sort on his head, like a circus performer. What the photograph did was trick out a stitch of highlights: hot points along the rod – it was a golf club, that was it – six, seven, and then one below, in the right eye of Tiger Woods. The photograph was about balance, and the balance had everything to do with the light in Tiger Woods's eye. Grandpa Gee had caught this. Would museum goers care? Would they get it?

CLICK.

A landscape. The colour hadn't fared well on this one, she knew. Was it Jason's journeyman mistake, back then, or was it her own glaucoma? Still, with its faults – the sugary blues, the fugitive reds – that rascally runaway brother of hers had started out strong. This was Tobago, when he'd finally got there. Some aberration of climate or some beginner's luck of Jason's had put him in the right place at the right time. A green fog had stolen in, midday, over the harbour. The wrong time of day for a fog! (Signs of things to come.) Probably Jason had staggered out of a drunken sleep to take a piss over the railing of his beachside shack, and been lucky enough to stumble upon an eerie landscape, and yet sober enough to recognize it. The photo showed one seashell, a conch of some sort – she used to know their names so well – resting on a beer can that rested on the railing. Beyond, the green fog from which poked up, like the tips of bulrushes, the lopsided masts of fishing boats. And above – the whole top two-thirds of the photo – a perfectly normal blue sky, with an industrialist's private jet coursing in from the mainland, heading for a dirty weekend with someone else's wife, or checking out the spooky water-smog. It was Magritte in Ektachrome. It was weird, accidental, and perfect. Jason was a genius. Lucky bastard.

CLICK.

Ah. One of her favourites. "Annie", it was called. On the back of the print was scribbled *Annie L.* But the L was crossed out, or scratched through. Maybe it signified the outdated symbol for sterling, the old British currency. A pound sign? Margaret had settled on "Annie" for the title, to be safe. Just in case there was an Annie L. who might show up at the exhibit, a hundred and sixty by now, and take offence. Because the photo was nothing short of luscious. An older woman, an aunt or guardian or mom, perhaps – Margaret had never known how to tell the difference – was clutching a girl whose long body flared out, like an eel, in spangles of light from a tidal pool. The pale buttocks were whorled with seaweed, and the hair was Pre-Raphaelitic in the extreme. Like Guinevere with her ivory finger in a light socket. The long hair almost disguised the fringe of lateral fin along the spine. But it couldn't mask the bed of shells against which the girl lay on her young and innocent breast. Margaret's eyes, drat them, grew damp looking at the loveliness, the birth of loveliness, its secret meaning. How had Gee *seen* all that?

CLICK.

From loveliness to forlornness. In the split of dark between one image and the next. Here was the portait called "Taro". A young Japanese lad dressed in the remains of a full-grown man's shirt – though the shirttails were knotted around his waist, and his pelvis was set on to a muddy track. He was shorn of his legs, for reasons Margaret could not remember – the history of wars in that century, so many, each so different, each so final, each not final enough! This portrait was a set-up, but so were the formal portraits of the crowned heads of Europe and Asia from the same period. Gee – or Taro himself, maybe – had arranged that two army boots be placed to one side of Taro's wheeled platform. They were shined, licorice-black, to within an inch of their lives. The laces were slung between them, knotted together to form a little airy sack. Dependent between them, like a Christmas bauble on display, hung a grenade. It was scored like a pineapple. Taro's hands, meanwhile, clutched his stumps, as if he was feeling to see if his toes had been driven three feet north into his hips. One eye looked at the camera. And then – how Gee got this shot! – the other eye looked right, off centre. Toward, though not right at, the grenade. Without turning, Taro couldn't actually see the still life of boots-and-grenade. He merely looked, as if imagining it must be there. As if he'd never be able to stop imagining it, and feeling for his toes.

The genius wasn't in the composition: it was in Gee's having seen that Taro's eyes could look in two directions at once, and working with that.

CLICK.

Not one of her own favourites, but a famous image. That

great heavyweight, what was his name? – the handsome man with the lustrous cocoa skin mugging next to the toothy grin of his pretend nemesis, some freckle-pocked Dubliner kid about ten or twelve. "Vee and Em" was the title Gee had given it. The public had admired it as a romp – the evident joy felt by its subjects kept the piece a perennial favourite. It had been reprinted in scores of photo anthologies of the century. A farce! Needle-nosed Irish scraper catching Mr Fame on the chin. (Muhammad Ali, that was his name.) What Margaret admired in this shot wasn't the fame of the image nor of its magnificent fighter hero, but the way that "Em" knew how to share the ring, honourably, with this pint-sized pugilist. This wasn't Youth and Age, or Novice and Champion, nothing so analogical or medievally schematic as that. To Margaret, the photo was one thing alone: the reverberation of charity – for each person was indulging the other. Charity seemed an endlessly renewable resource in this photo. It was as if Gee was saying: stop hunting for *perpetual motion*, and start thinking *perpetual motions*. Only in duality is movement possible. Oh, those two grins, of Vee and Em! She loved them so, even if the photo had become so famous as to deteriorate into cliché.

CLICK.

The one of Chantal and Jacqueline. It pained Margaret to see this, even now, and she nearly forwarded past it. Still, how many more times would she be able to look at it? She had included it in this collection in order to gain control over it, to slight it by insisting it was ordinary, categorizable. The photographer, after all, was George Keane. Somehow. He must have shot this a year or so before he died. It was a grainy black and white, shot in low natural light. Dusk in Provence in the barren months. You could almost hear the mistral. Jacqueline was blurred, sitting in the background with her round, beloved head tilted against a wall. Her eyes were shut as if resting, or listening to a broadcast. The right-hand third of Chantal's image, nearer, bled off the margin of the print. An old-fashioned telephone handset was cradled between her neck and ear. A pencil waited in her hand, midair. A soft, half-eaten croissant dangled from her mouth. The opened, vulnerable pastry resembled nothing so much as a soft-sculpture of a seashell. This was clearly an intimate photo of women by a photographer who had loved them personally. In the absence of a given title, Margaret had called it "News".

CLICK.

Oh. Her very favourite. "Lev". The flattened chin and bruised nose of the subject in the cell's middle-distance: the incarcerate, poor blighter. His face was mostly in shadow but for a strand of glossy saliva, yoking cracked upper lip to lower. In the background, half-lit but out of focus, a calendar with a caption in, it seemed, Cyrillic script. Foreground: the box. Her box. Held up at right angles to the floor – by Lev's fingers, probably, though they weren't apparent. Not yet finished with carved lids nor silk linings; just a box of seven chambers. The squares of the box were empty, echoing the squares of the calendar page. Empty. The face between them, though, was full.

That's where the box had come from. Where had it gone? She couldn't remember.

CLICK.

"High Vincentia". The last photo of Jason's, taken only minutes before his transport vessel lost power and disappeared off the radar. The title derived from the computer identity of the coordinates; the image was of nothing so recognizable as a town or a landing strip, a beach or a bazaar. Ten years before, she'd gone there herself: she'd been drawn out of grief for his death, and confusion about the image. He had never indulged in photographic tricks beyond those of lighting and composition; he'd never acceded to the reality of the digital edit, pixel by pixel, fact by fact. "That's painting by number," he'd said. "I paint by light, mercury, and shadow."

So what was the last image of? – the image he could never explain, for he'd disappeared a few moments later? Analysts had been unable to explain the phenomenon recorded on the sensors, even imagining every useful sort of equipment malfunction. Another – the fifth or sixth such in his long life – of the weird atmospheric conundrums he'd been lucky enough to make a reputation for recording. There was the curve of the earth – the vehicle had been coming in from quite an orbit – and there, like silk submerged in water, a shoal of fish picked out in sequins of grey silver. A single cloud like a lazy question mark on its side coiling above what she imagined must be High Vincentia. But the cloud showed twice. If you didn't look carefully, you might think that one was the shadow of the other. Looking more carefully, though, the shadow was differently shaped – so, was it a shadow, or a thing unto itself? How the dickens had Jason seen it? Caught it on film? What did he think it meant? It was like a closed system of referents between clouds – *one* of them ought to have cast a shadow on the water below, but neither did. It was almost as if the lower cloud had caught the shadow of the upper, and by it been changed into something new.

He'd seen this. The Logometer had recorded a comment. "Prior infinity," he'd said, though whether colloquially, sardonically, or reverentially could not be deduced. "The choices aren't conditional any longer, and they're not exclusive."

His body had never been found nor, for that matter, the vehicle.

CLICK.

There were others. Some of Iona's. Nice enough. A start anyway. More famous ones of Gee's: JFK, Hollytan Skerling, the Mendocino Nine. Juvenile ones of Jason's: the glass series. Shapes of things to come! Then, two portraits of herself, looking vapid and young. As she still felt, after all this time.

They began to blur. She should sharpen the focus.

* * *

She hadn't known she was asleep. She woke up suddenly – glad, as always she was, to wake up at all. The girl was arranging clothes on the bed.

"The black – not the wool – the other one," said Margaret.

"You're awake. I hope I didn't disturb you. It's daylight."

It was. Once again, it was daylight. How brilliant.

"Look," said Margaret, "um, look." The girl, her name – *Iona*, that was it. "Iona. Over here."

Margaret pushed her air-chair up – it had sunk into a resting position, half-cocked in the air when it had sensed her falling asleep – and she rotated it around the corner of the bed to where her small suitcase stood open on a stand. "I have something for you."

Iona stood aside with her hands in her sweater pockets. *Why did they wear such ugly baggy sweaters, the young? Never mind: Do what you're doing.*

She fished about in her jewellery case and found what she wanted.

"Come here, Iona, dear. I have a present I've been saving for many years."

Iona said, "I don't want anything from you, Meggsie – Maggie, I mean."

"Oh, come on; Meggsie will do. I'm used to it. No, come here."

"I didn't mean it, about 'leaving' me anything. You have left me dozens of memories. Hundreds." Oh, so the sweater was to keep a wodge of paper handkerchief.

"What are you getting weepy about? You did *not* get the sleep you needed, young lady. I know the symptoms well. Now, come here as I tell you to."

Iona approached. Margaret held out her hand and gave her the last shell.

"This belonged to your great-great-grandfather, Gee," said Margaret. "He left it to me with instructions that I was to throw it back. Throw it into the sea, I suppose he meant. That's what I did with the others. But the last one – well, I couldn't. I suppose I just needed to disobey. After all, I have the Keane gene too."

She flashed a wicked smile; Iona couldn't help but smile back.

"He wanted us to see," said Margaret. "That was his legacy. He gave his grandson – your grandfather – a camera, and he gave me a set of shells. Jason took the camera and took off – his life took off. He saw through the lens. He learned to adjust the aperture, to see as keenly as the instrument allows. I took the shells and I took off too, and wandered the world, and saw what came my way. That's all we ever want to give away, you know. Not really ourselves, not even our genes. Just our hopes that the young will remember to look, and to see. Through whatever means possible."

"What should I do with the shell?" asked Iona.

"I couldn't care less what you do with it," said Margaret. "I've finished my job. I've tossed it to you. You toss it back now, or later. Or never. Scandalous profusion of choices.

Infinite directions. Your shot. You pick the focal depth. It's your turn."

THE
EN D

ABOUT THE AUTHORS

Linda Sue Park (Chapter One: Maggie) won the Newbery Medal for *A Single Shard*. Her most recent books are *Project Mulberry*, *Archer's Quest*, and *Tap Dancing on the Roof*. She has competed in gymnastic meets (as a college student), cook-offs, and on *Jeopardy!* (in 2006). Linda Sue lives with her family in western New York.

David Almond (Chapter Two: Annie) won the Printz Award for *Kit's Wilderness* and the Carnegie Medal for *Skellig*, his first novel. His other books include *Heaven Eyes*, *Secret Heart*, *The Fire-Eaters*, *Clay*, and the short-story collection *Counting Stars*. A two-time winner of the Whitbread Children's Book Award, he lives in Northumberland, in the north of England.

Eoin Colfer (Chapter Three: Jason) is the author of five books in the bestselling *Artemis Fowl* series, as well as *The Supernaturalist*, *Half-Moon Investigations*, *The Wish List*, *Benny and Omar*, and *Benny and Babe*. His one-man show *Artemis Fowl: Fairies, Fiends, and Flatulence* played to enthusiastic audiences in London's West End in the autumn of 2006. He lives in Wexford, Ireland.

Deborah Ellis (Chapter Four: Lev) won the Governor General's Award for her first novel, *Looking for X*. After spending time in Pakistan interviewing Afghan refugees, she wrote a trilogy based on the experiences of women and children she met there: *The Breadwinner*, *Parvana's Journey*, and *Mud City*. Her other books have dealt with kids affected by AIDS in Africa, and kids caught up in the war between Israel and Palestine. She lives in Simcoe, Canada.

Nick Hornby (Chapter Five: Maggie) is the author of four novels, two essay collections (on pop music and books), and a memoir. Three of his books have been made into movies, one of them twice: *Fever Pitch*, *High Fidelity* and *About a Boy*. He lives in Highbury, in north London, England, where he cheers for the Arsenal soccer team.

Roddy Doyle (Chapter Six: Vincent) won the Booker Prize for *Paddy Clarke Ha Ha Ha*. He has written seven adult novels – most recently *Paula Spencer* – and four books for young readers, including *The Giggler Treatment*, *Rover Saves Christmas*, *The Meanwhile Adventures*, and *Wilderness*. He lives in Dublin, Ireland.

Tim Wynne-Jones (Chapter Seven: Min) has twice won the Governor General's Award for Fiction, for *The Maestro* and *Some of the Kinder Planets*. His other novels include *Rex Zero and the End of the World*, *A Thief in the House of Memory*,

The Boy in the Burning House, and *Stephen Fair*. He cooks and does the *New York Times* crossword puzzle near Perth, Ontario, Canada.

Ruth Ozeki (Chapter Eight: Jiro) is the author of two novels, *My Year of Meats* and *All Over Creation*, both named *New York Times* Notable Books. *My Year of Meats* also won the Kiriyama Pacific Rim Prize. A former filmmaker and television director, Ruth now divides her time between New York City and British Columbia, where she writes, knits socks, and raises exotic Chinese chickens.

Margo Lanagan (Chapter Nine: Afela) is the author of three collections of extraordinary short stories, *Black Juice*, *White Time*, and *Red Spikes*, among fourteen other books. *Black Juice* won a Printz Honor and a World Fantasy Award for best collection, and was shortlisted for the *Los Angeles Times* Book Prize. Margo lives in Sydney, Australia.

Gregory Maguire (Chapter Ten: Margaret) has written twenty-five books for children and adults, many reflecting his fascinations with fairy tales and other popular myths, including *Confessions of an Ugly Stepsister*; *Mirror, Mirror*; and *Leaping Beauty*. His novel *Wicked* was adapted for a popular Broadway musical. Gregory lives outside Boston, Massachusetts.

ABOUT AMNESTY INTERNATIONAL

Amnesty International is a movement of ordinary people from across the world standing up for humanity and human rights. Our purpose is to protect individuals wherever justice, fairness, freedom and truth are denied.

Human rights are basic principles that allow people to live dignified lives, free from abuse, fear and want, and free to express their own beliefs. Human rights belong to all of us, whoever we are and wherever we live. And our human rights are recognized in all the countries of the world by the Universal Declaration of Human Rights and international law.

Human rights are why the authors of *Click* could write this book. Human rights mean you can read it. In some countries people are imprisoned and even tortured for expressing their ideas in writing or for daring to support Amnesty International. You could even be imprisoned for reading a book like this.

Amnesty International started in 1961. Today, nearly half a century later, we have over two million members in 150 countries around the world. In the UK and Ireland we have an active membership, including hundreds of youth and student groups. You can join us as an individual member, link up with one of our local or youth groups, or start up a group yourself. Youth groups are gatherings of young people in schools, sixth form colleges or youth clubs, who meet to campaign for Amnesty International. They hold publicity stunts, write letters to government leaders and officials, fundraise, get publicity in their local papers, hold assemblies and create displays. Whether you join individually or as part of a group, we can send you magazines and letter-writing actions.

If you would like to join Amnesty International, set up a group or simply find out more, please contact:

Amnesty International UK
The Human Rights Action Centre
17-25 New Inn Yard,
London EC2A 3EA
Tel: 020 7033 1500
Email: sct@amnesty.org.uk
www.amnesty.org.uk

or

Amnesty International Ireland
Sean MacBride House,
48 Fleet St.
Dublin 2,
Ireland
Tel: (+353 1) 677 6361
Email: info@amnesty.ie
www.amnesty.ie

Since Amnesty International started, people have written letters on behalf of victims of human rights abuses. Today, hundreds of thousands of ordinary people throughout the world challenge cruelty and injustice by taking a few minutes to write a letter.

"It is impossible to paint an accurate picture of [my] reactions as I sat in that tiny cell, the floor carpeted with cards and envelopes, generated through Amnesty's efforts. It was deeply touching, greatly encouraging and strengthening. . . I knew that I was not alone. . . Maybe you just send one card – but all of these cards are like little drops of water that combine to create an avalanche of pressure. . . It was so moving. I gained such strength from them. I knew I had committed no crime and now I knew the world also knew why I was in prison."

Chris Anyanwu, Nigerian journalist and Amnesty International prisoner of conscience. She received 9,000 cards from Amnesty members.